One for the Road

By Jeremy M. Moore

Dedication:

To Kim, my wife, who never stopped believing in me.

To all my friends and family who supported me through the years.

To all who have gone before me, I hope we share a drink again soon.

Table of Contents

Chapter 1: Shelter from the Heat

"Where am I?" Miguel wheezed through his parched throat. Sweat stung his eyes as he baked under an unforgiving sun, and a scalding wind whipped around him. Sand blasted against him, raking across sunburnt skin. *Hurts… it hurts to be out here. Where* is *here?* He tried turning his neck, but his muscles would not respond. His body resisted his commands in this nightmare environment. For a moment, he wondered if that defiance was to protect him from this place or to condemn him to remain.

As the pain from the sun, wind, and sand grew, he fought to turn his head to accomplish even that small goal. His muscles tensed, a groan rattled in his chest, but his body refused to comply with his will. Miguel kept applying pressure, his moans growing louder as he fought himself. *Am I paralyzed? Is that possible while standing? How is that possible?*

The internal battle between his mind and body went on for what felt like hours in these hellish conditions until Miguel felt a snap inside him and a chill ran through him. It was like a dam had broken and sent ice-cold water into every corner of his body. With that victory, he found he could turn his neck, although even that motion took great effort. Still, it allowed him to complete his survey of his surroundings. It was a barren location, a dusty, broken land. As far as he could see in every direction, there was nothing but dry, shattered ground and a yellow, cloudless sky.

Only one thing marred the lifeless expanse: a small, weathered shack worn down by years of exposure to this harsh environment. In defiance of the elements, it stood. While it did not look to be sturdy or safe, Miguel felt compelled to enter. If nothing else, it would get him out of this heat. *Stepping on a nail or a flimsy board would be better than being out here.*

Each step was a chore, every footfall a hard thud that further cracked the shattered ground. The heat stole his energy with every movement, nibbling away at his stamina, but he pushed onward. His joints ground together as sweat poured down his face. Miguel reached the battered and broken landing and collapsed, the rough wood scraping his hands. The weather-beaten roof offered little shade, and the few remaining boards creaked in the wind. Grabbing the smooth black door handle, he chastised himself for not thinking it would scald him. Enduring the pain, he grasped the handle and shoved.

Nothing happened.

Despite its faded and battered appearance, the door refused to budge even an inch. "Please," he whispered. "I need to be inside. I can't stay out here." The heat seared his back, and he wondered if he would soon ignite like tinder in a campfire. He continued shoving the door handle and used his free hand to push on the door itself. Nothing was moving. The old door remained in its place. "Just open for me, please. I'd do anything to be out of this heat." With the last of his strength, Miguel put his shoulder to the door and shoved.

The door swung open with a resounding bang as it collided with the shack's inner wall. "Success," Miguel spat as he staggered into the dingy building. There were no lights, or even a light switch that Miguel could see, but the interior was small enough that the light shining in through the door allowed him to take stock of his surroundings. The old building appeared to be the ruins of a small bar. At its maximum, the entire place could never have held more than a dozen people. There were no hallways or side rooms, just a simple rectangular room. All that broke it up were two small round wooden tables with old, warped chairs and the bar itself, a crude, wooden rise with bolted-down high-backed chairs. Despite the rough design, it appeared sturdy, and right now, Miguel needed something stable.

Doesn't matter what this place is or used to be. As long as it gets me out of this heat.

From inside the door, Miguel glanced back into the heat. He had lived his entire life in warm climates, but never anything like he had experienced out there. This brought questions to mind. *Where did I live? Also, where am I now?* Struggling to focus, Miguel could not recall much. His memories were there, and he knew who he was, but every thought was hiding under a layer of fog.

Scanning the horizon, Miguel confirmed no other buildings, or even the remains of other buildings, anywhere in sight. Not even the signs of a road. *No road? But I was crossing the road to my car. I was picking up...* Miguel stopped. The memory had risen to the forefront of his mind and now sank back into the mental fog. *What was I doing? How did I get here?* His head swam with images: grabbing a plastic bag, making small talk with someone behind a counter, a phone call, and him moving into the road. *Then...*

Confusion shifted to panic. *Why am I here? Where is here? I was at a... at the store, right? But now —*

Miguel's head spun as fatigue washed over him. The heat had taken its toll, making even the simple act of thinking nearly impossible.

He moved out of the doorway, his footfalls coming in rapid succession. There was a feeling of someone or something shoving him farther inside. A twinge of fear crawled up his spine as he took in his new surroundings.

Behind him, the stubborn door creaked closed, casting enormous shadows around the room. Since he had seen nothing alive in the bar, Miguel allowed himself to relax. He was safe. Or at least safer than he had been outside. A part of him fought against moving any farther inside—that rebellious spark wanting to remain a few steps past the door so he could easily flee back into the light—but his aching legs cried out for relief, and Miguel pushed his fear aside as he shambled toward the bar.

Every step was a struggle, and he threw himself forward at a hobble. *Now that I am out of the heat, I can rest a minute. Maybe then I can... I can think. Call... Call who?* The wheels of his mind ground to a halt. For the life of him, he could recall nothing. The same questions echoed in his mind.

Miguel looked at his right hand, trying to flex his fingers, which reacted as if they were holding some unseen object. *Didn't I have a bag?* When he peered back at the door, a single beam of light still slipped through. *I could go back out and find my bag. It might help me get some answers.*

Before he could turn, however, he collided with a barstool. Miguel winced at the abrupt stop, rubbing his ribs. *That was closer than I thought. Well, sit first. Then I'll go bag-hunting.* Aches and pains ran up and down his limbs, and he fought just to sit upon that chair. Miguel stabilized himself against its back, wincing as the touch of the chair stung his sunburnt skin. Even through his shirt, he felt the coarse wood. Despite it all, he let out a final, exhausted sigh of comfort. As much pain as this ordeal had caused him, sitting in the cool darkness was far better than standing in the heat. "Perhaps things are looking up. I mean, I'm still alive. That's a start, right?" He tried to laugh, to find some reassurance in his own words, but he could only cough.

Is that really your best advice, Miguel?

The thought popped into his mind like someone else was speaking in his thoughts. “Hello,” he wheezed into the darkness. No response came, and he smiled to himself. “Guess it was the bar talking to me. Either that or I’ve gone crazy.” He inspected the room, confirming he was alone. The door gave off a final click as it closed. With the sun’s heat cut off by the shack’s heavy wooden door, the room’s temperature dropped. The heat dissipated, consumed by the room’s chill, and numbness moved through his body, dulling the aches and pains. Exhausted, he swayed in his seat.

All he wanted was to rest, to let go, to stop. Miguel laid his head on the coarse bar, enjoying its steady structure. With a lengthy sigh, he closed his eyes and allowed himself to drift away.

Chapter 2: Opening the Bar

Miguel was not sure how long he had been resting against the counter, but a fit of rasping coughs shook him out of his peaceful respite. "Probably too much to hope that the bar still has anything to drink," he mused, hoping that by speaking the words he might make them come true.

A drink in a place like this? Impossible. Melancholy seeped into him, nibbling away at the agitated energy caused by his hacking. It chipped away at each of his senses, replacing desire with apathy. He was so tired. A numbing weakness moved into his arms and legs. Miguel shrank into his mind, retreating further and deeper into those thoughts. "Just… so… tired… and thirsty…"

Thunk.

Something firm struck the space before him, shaking him from his dour thoughts. It was not that the building was settling, and there had been nothing around him that could have fallen over. He opened his eyes, expecting only empty darkness. Instead, on the bar before him sat a cold, frosted glass filled to the brim with amber liquid. Like in a commercial, the drink glistened in the light as a bead of moisture flowed down the side.

Is this a mirage? Am I so dehydrated that I'm seeing glowing drinks? With apprehension, his hands hovered over the glass. *If I grab it, does it just mean I've gone crazy?*

To his great pleasure and relief, it did not vanish, and his hands clasped around the smooth, wet glass. A refreshing chill spread from his chapped hands, and the dry ache faded. It soothed his skin, the sensation running up his arms and into his chest. He sighed, this time without coughing. With that cool touch came an old memory: the first time he and his wife, Vanessa, went to the park for a picnic. He could recall it all with crystal clarity. She spun, a long smile on her face as they walked, letting her striped sundress twirl in the summer breeze coming off the lake. The wind would catch her hat and carry it away. No matter how many times it happened, she would let out a surprised shriek and he would run off to retrieve the errant hat. He remembered how happy it made her and how she would reward him with a kiss on the cheek. All of this happening during a refreshing summer breeze. Miguel chuckled at that memory. *We were so young back then. Before things got complicated. That was one of our first dates.*

Vanessa. He winced as more memories of his wife pierced his mental fog. Other dates flashed in his mind's eye: their wedding day and the time they had spent with loved ones. He could make out details about Vanessa, no one else, but he knew the figures there were important to him. *How could I forget her, even for a moment?* His head ached. *What was that? Why am I having so much trouble remembering things?* He spun the wet glass in his hands, enjoying its cool surface against his injured skin. *It happened when I touched this beer.*

"Wait… where did this come from? Drinks don't just appear. How?" He stopped, focusing on the drink. Light shone beyond it, but the front door had been the only source of illumination. "What…?"

"Drink," a harsh voiced interrupted. "Ya know, glug, glug, down the hatch, one for the road, and all that."

Miguel jumped, almost falling from his chair. Behind what he knew had been an empty bar was a woman dressed in an immaculate black and white bartender's uniform. Staring him dead in the eyes, she made a repeated pouring motion toward her mouth while jabbing a finger at the drink. "Drink," she slurred, dragging out the word. When he did not mimic her motions, she raised an eyebrow. "What, do people not do that anymore?"

Miguel wanted to respond but was too dumbstruck by her sudden appearance to do anything. Here, in this broken-down remnant of a bar, stood an attractive woman with neat, shoulder-length black hair tied back with a simple red ribbon, bronze skin, and amber eyes that reflected the bar's lights. For a moment, a flash of crimson spilled over the surface of her eyes. She stopped her pouring and pointing motions, letting out a growl that deflated into a sigh. "Why does it always have to go down like this?" she asked with a glance to the ceiling. Their eyes met, locking in place. A growing pressure built all over his body, her glare pushing him into his seat. Her words rolled out with the slow and deliberate power of a coming storm, each one a lightning strike against his heart.

"Do. Not. Be. Afraid."

Miguel wheezed, his heart fluttering in his chest as a mixture of growing relief and fading fear churned in his stomach.

"Oh, come on. It's not that bad. Just focus," she complained as he swayed. Three versions of the bartender swam in his vision.

Are each of them doing something different? Shaking his head, which only made things spin a little more, he studied the amber drink on the counter, glad to have something still to steady his focus. Miguel did not look up for several moments, trying to just breathe and think, but he could feel her glare upon him the entire time. She seemed to be sizing him up, perhaps worried he would become a bigger problem for her.

When the room stopped spinning, the bartender became just one image again, and his insides stopped gurgling. Miguel let out a final, loud breath. While her presence still confused him, he had to admit that he was no longer feeling fear or panic. Now that he possessed a little more mental clarity, questions formed in his mind. He wanted to ask the bartender where he was, what had happened to him, and where she had come from, but he asked, "How did you give me this drink from over there? I didn't hear you pour it or slide it over." He glanced from her to where he sat, rubbing a hand over the counter, a splinter poking his finger. Miguel winced, pulling the wood from the injured digit. "I don't think you *could* slide anything on this counter."

"Whatever. For someone just coughing for a drink, you sure like to talk when you should be drinking. All you need to know is I am the bartender." She paused, spreading her hands and gesturing to the area in front of her. "Y'know, tending bar. Getting drinks to people who need them."

As she made her mocking presentation, a light illuminating the bar caught Miguel's attention; it had not been there when he first rested his head. When he sat down, it had just been a dingy wooden counter with some old but sturdy wooden stools. Now there were a variety of beer taps running the length of the bar and a full rack of liquors and wines along the wall. *Surely, I should have at least seen them. How out of it am I?* He also noted that the stools were now plush red seats with chrome-covered bases. Even the one he sat upon no longer had the coarse backing.

I'm sure there was a back to the chair. Didn't I use the back to help get on it? His mind whirled as he tried reconciling what he remembered with what he was seeing. *I came into a rundown shack, with everything made of rotten wood and covered in dust. Yet here they are, as plain as the nose on my face.* Miguel tapped his nose, checking that it was still on his face. He scanned the room in case he had missed anything else, but everything around him appeared as he remembered it: filthy and falling apart.

The bartender slapped her cleaning rag on the counter, nodding to the frosty drink before Miguel. He followed her motion. "Look, let's make it simple. You wanted a drink. I served you. You came in thirsty. Probably dehydrated, right? I put down a drink, and you just didn't see it. So what's the problem here? You drink like a person, don't you?"

"Yes, but—"

"Then drink and take comfort," she declared with an odd flourish, almost as if she was imitating a speech he should know. Despite how flowery she made the words, Miguel understood her patience had reached its end. "If you're drinking, you aren't asking me dumb questions."

Miguel nodded, his scratchy throat eager for anything to drink. He reached for the glass, then hesitated before setting it back on the counter. "Wait a minute."

"What is it now?" The bartender sighed with a roll of her eyes.

"I don't have my wallet. I can't pay for this."

"It's on the house." She waved off his words before moving to the bar's opposite end. It was a short walk but conveyed her desire to leave the conversation. "All drinks are complimentary here."

"Oh, well, thank you then. That's very…" He stopped as she shot him another fierce glare. Raising the glass toward her, he nodded. "As you said, one for the road, yes?" The drink's scent hit him first. For a moment, his thoughts cleared. Memories rose from the depths of his mind. He remembered meals with coworkers to celebrate successes and the end of a long work week. A drink with friends to relieve tension. Miguel smiled. *What an odd thing to remember. I must tell them about it when I get back. After I tell Vanessa, that is.*

"Vanessa," he whispered, lowering the untouched drink as an idea came to mind. "Do you have a phone I can use? I need to call my wife. Please, it's important."

The bartender did not turn, paying no attention to him. However, Miguel noticed that she was putting extra effort into wiping the glass in her hand. Any harder and he was certain the glass would shatter under the pressure. “No outside line,” she growled before adding, “And what did I say about drinking and not asking stupid questions?”

“But—” He stopped as she whirled on him. Miguel thought he must have blinked or momentarily looked away, because she was standing a hair’s breadth from him, somehow having cleared the distance without him seeing her move. Her amber eyes flared, red sparks flaring across them, and he melted away from her.

“Drink,” she commanded, and his arm started lifting the glass again, as if obeying her orders were its natural reaction. “Everything will work itself out. You need to just do what I told you. Take. A. Drink.”

So much for friendly customer service. Again, the drink's scent brought back memories, this time of his office. The office itself was not special, a simple rental space in a strip mall, but he remembered all the effort he and his team had put into it. All that hard work to make it a welcoming place for their clients. The thoughts broke his concentration and his arm lowered the beverage. "Are you sure I can't at least call my office? Let them know where I am? They can call Vanessa, my wife, for me. I have clients that count on me to—"

"Drink," she snarled. "I'm tired of repeating myself. I've got a lot to do and can't spend all night playing with a human."

If I'm only a human, what does that make you? A few choice descriptors came to mind, but Miguel shook his head, dismissing the thoughts. She leaned in closer, her displeasure at his defiance clear in the scowl on her face, and he was not sure what she would do next.

“Well, you see, I’m expected back at work. People depend on me. There are clients who need my help.” Miguel paused. Again, his hand rose with the drink, but this time there was no sensation of lifting it. The beverage and his hand seemed to rise of their own accord. *No, it’s the bartender.* She had placed one finger on the bottom of his glass and lifted it toward his mouth. Realizing she would not relent, he sighed. *Okay, one sip. Then maybe she’ll listen to reason.* After a quick glance at her grim expression, he amended his thoughts. *Reason might be out of the question, but she might at least listen.*

The amber liquid flowed to the edge of the glass, brushing against his dry lips with the promise of cool, wet comfort. But before he could take that first sip, a resounding thud filled the air.

Miguel looked to the entrance, expecting it to be wide open again. A few drops of amber liquid spilled onto the counter, and the bartender removed her finger to clean the spilled beverage, complaining about how no one appreciated what went into making an excellent drink. Miguel missed most of her string of criticisms; he was more concerned with what was happening at the front door. But he found himself confused by the lack of anything happening. The door remained closed, with no sign of anyone having entered the room. *So where did that noise come from?*

"Expecting a visitor?" Someone laughed over his shoulder. Miguel jolted and would have fallen off his stool if his brain could decide which direction it wanted to run. Instead, he flailed in place. "You're a jumpy little guy, eh?"

Beside Miguel was a chubby man dressed head to toe in a crisp, dark blue suit with a matching hat and tie accented by his hot pink shirt. He smiled, his white teeth glistening so much in the bar light that Miguel expected a tiny star to shine on them. The man exuded confidence with every motion. "It's all right, amigo." He nodded. "You have nothing to fear from me."

"I already told him not to be afraid," the bartender snarled.

"Really?" the man said, resting his hat and jacket on the bar as he took the seat beside Miguel. "Are you losing your touch, Raquel?"

"You nearly gave me a heart attack," Miguel whimpered, rubbing his chest. "Where did you even come from?"

The man held three fingers toward the bartender. "Not possible," he replied without concern. "In fact, I can honestly tell you that such a thing will not happen to you here. Trust me on that, amigo. Still, it is always good to know you have a heart, yes?"

Beads of sweat on the man's head glistened in the bar's light. *Did he come in from outside, too? Why didn't I see* him *out there? Is there something behind the bar? That would make sense. Could there be an office back there?*

Raquel shook her head at his three fingers. In a fluid motion, she slammed a shot glass down, produced a bottle from beneath the bar, flipped it, and poured out a drink. The man watched with excitement, licking his lips in anticipation, but pouted when she stopped short. "Two," she declared, holding up a matching number of fingers. "You were off-key last night."

The man reacted as if she had reached out and struck him. He made an exaggerated sweeping motion with his arms, knocking his hat from the counter and onto a seat beside him.

Wait, wasn't he in the last chair?

"Off-key? Why would you say something so cruel? When has Juan Pedro *ever* been off-key?"

"Cry in your drink," she snapped, sliding over the shot. "I've got a good ear for music."

Miguel ignored their bickering and ran a cautious hand on the counter. *She slid a drink to him. I got a splinter from this counter, and now it's as smooth as glass.* The counter was not glass, but he found it was a wood polished to a sheen. *What? How?*

"Ah, yes, your last job," Juan Pedro mused and raised his shot glass high in the air. "To another perfect night." He downed the contents of his glass, slammed it on the bar, and let out the loudest, most satisfied sigh Miguel had ever heard.

Even drinking is a production with this man.

"Nothing like a bit of liquid happiness to start us off, yes?" Juan Pedro purred, reaching over to give Miguel a gentle pat on the shoulder. He gave the bartender a polite nod of thanks and leaned in close to Miguel as if to whisper but continued in his normal baritone. "Raquel provides the best service with a scowl."

The bartender grunted with little enthusiasm, showing more interest in removing the empty shot glass and resuming her cleaning of the glass from earlier.

Juan Pedro offered Miguel a mischievous smile, nodding in her direction. "Between you and me, if it were not for the wonderful drinks she serves, I would not put up with her abuse. I could find work elsewhere, you know. Juan Pedro is drawn to the stage, but the stage exists for Juan Pedro. It is my talent that draws in the crowds."

Miguel said nothing, trying to figure out if Juan Pedro was insane or unaware of how scary Raquel could be. *If this is some game between them, I want out.* "I, um… Do you know where I can find a phone? See, I need to call my wife. She—"

"What is this?" Juan Pedro blurted in dismay. He wrapped one arm around Miguel, gesturing toward the drink on the counter like he had discovered a buried treasure filled with precious gems. "You haven't touched your drink. My friend, uh…" He paused, his brow furrowing.

"Miguel."

"Miguel," he repeated with deep approval and a hint of reverence. "Miguel, a fine name. It means 'in God's image,' yes? That makes you a man of importance and wisdom. One of *fine* taste." Juan Pedro nodded, agreeing with himself but not giving Miguel any time to speak. "Well, my friend, my godly named friend, I *must* know something." He made a sweeping gesture to the counter. "Tell me, were you so enamored by the beautiful señorita that you could not bring yourself to drink?"

"Well, I was about to drink when—"

Juan Pedro dismissed Miguel's comment with a shake of his hand. "No, no, no, Miguel. Raquel." He twirled a hand to the bartender. "She is not your type. Trust me on this. No, my friend, you must focus not on chasing far-off goals but on finishing what is before you. Drink the drink provided. Do not pine for the bottle on the highest shelf. A drink such as this." Juan Pedro picked up Miguel's drink, holding it to the ceiling's bright lights.

When did those appear? Miguel wondered before being drawn back in by Juan Pedro's theatrics.

"A drink, a fine drink like this… Well, it's something to enjoy, to savor, even when served by a woman as tone-deaf as our barkeep."

Raquel responded by halving a series of limes with a smooth motion, never taking her eyes off Juan Pedro. Miguel got the impression that glare was a thinly veiled threat for both of them, despite his silence during the interaction. Juan Pedro continued, unfazed. “A drink like this. It is cold, refreshing, and satisfying. I understand your deep consideration, my friend, your wistful silence and desire to *savor* it. Life is like this drink, full-bodied and exciting, and you wonder what happens when it is gone, yes? When you finish, what comes next? Will this one be enough for the road ahead?” In one quick, well-practiced motion, he drained the contents of Miguel’s drink and again let out a sigh of immense satisfaction. He clapped Miguel on his sunburnt back before returning the glass to the counter. “Do not waste your night thinking such deep thoughts. Do not regret or lament the drinks of the past. Stay in the here and now and enjoy all the night has to offer. Tonight comes along only once in a lifetime, yes? Drinks, like ourselves, can be refilled.”

Staring at his now-empty glass, Miguel took a moment to process what had happened. His drink was empty. The same drink that, mere moments ago, he had held up to his lips. His throat ached, and he considered trying to get those last few drops. They would not be much, but any amount of the amber liquid could only help soothe his raspy throat.

Before he could act, Raquel collected the empty vessel and tossed it into a container under the bar. Miguel's face flushed with anger as he turned in the direction Juan Pedro had walked, ready to demand that the larger man replace his drink.

"Excuse me," he barked but stopped as he noticed that the room's appearance had once again changed. Juan Pedro, who was now carrying an instrument case, approached a small stage at the far wall. *Where did all that come from? Was it all behind a drop cloth? No, there was nothing there when I showed up. I know it. I am sure it didn't look like this.*

"What the hell is going on here?" Frustration overwhelmed his confusion. The bartender took an angry breath, rising to her full height. Confused by her reaction, Miguel cast a glance at Raquel, but instead of seeing her, he noticed that the walls had become smooth and painted, a better fit for her station. Even the floor had changed and was no longer made up of warped board and rotten planks. Instead, the flooring was now straight and polished to a sheen. Overhead lights illuminated multiple round tables now scattered all over the room. *What is going on?* Panic slipped back into his voice. "What the hell is—ow!"

Raquel's hand pulled back slowly, the quick jab to his upper arm causing Miguel to let out a whimper. "Stop saying that. It's bad luck and disrespectful to the hosts."

Tears welled in the corners of his eyes, and he groaned in pain. Again, Raquel had moved without him seeing, as she had returned to her preparations at the other end of the bar.

What is happening to me? Giving his arm a weak rotation, Miguel tried to ignore the pain and focus on asking questions. "Saying what? How big is this place? Are the lights not all on? Where am I? Why does this place look like it keeps getting bigger?"

"Always more questions with you," Raquel muttered. "I already told you to not be afraid, so stop it. It's not our fault you're…" She stopped, reacting to something over Miguel's shoulder. "You're here," she finished, not sounding happy with the words.

"You are in my establishment," a slow, sultry voice cooed from behind him, "and it is as big as it needs to be. Perfect for the night in question."

Miguel rose from his chair, prepared to throw all his frustration at the speaker. In this place were a bartender who threatened and assaulted him and a musician who stole his drinks, and he was too tired for any more riddles and mind games. If this was the owner, she would get an earful of his complaints. Miguel might not know where he was, but he would not be silent any longer. “This has gone on long enough. No more making a fool of me. I…” The words caught in his throat and he stopped walking after taking a few steps from the bar. The hostess descended the last few steps of a wooden staircase. Miguel could just make out the new floor behind her, which looked more like a hotel than the upper level of any bar he had ever seen. *Is that where everyone came from? But then when did the second floor appear?*

Things shimmered and changed around the new woman. The closer she drew, the more organized and neater the room became, as though she gave definition to it, like she was ink lines on a colored image. *What the hell is going on?* He winced, expecting Raquel to react to his thoughts and hit him again for asking the question. When she did not, he turned back to the woman.

A memory flashed in the front of his mind, but he had no recollection of what it meant. Something about this woman stirred a recollection deep in his mind, but the thought was elusive and fled before he could identify it. *What was that?*

Unlike Raquel and her dour demeanor, this woman had a welcoming presence. Her steel-gray eyes captivated him, giving him a still feeling of peaceful rest, as if he could relax and let go of his cares. Like the bartender, there was a small motion across her eyes; small flecks of green popped over their surface before fading away. Her straight dark hair flowed in an unseen breeze, bouncing as she walked. Miguel's heart raced when he gazed at her tanned skin and full, red lips. The woman was lovely, beautiful in an unsettling way, yet he could not help but look at her.

Miguel noticed she wore a fiery red dress. This was not a metaphor. Her dress was literally on fire, slowly burning from the hem upward. Long tongues of rainbow-colored flame tried to pull every fiber of cloth into its starving maw.

She neither noticed nor acknowledge that she was aflame, something Miguel would have prioritized. The flames must have been burning for at least a few minutes, as they were now mid-calf with no signs of slowing. Where it had passed, the fabric had become black but did not leave a brittle char or ashen color. Instead, the fire only appeared to change the red silken fabric to one of black velvet.

Wisps of smoke rose from the flickering flames, reaching out to her bare arms and face. Where they touched, small obsidian flecks started to form into a design, a pattern Miguel could not yet place.

"You are on fire," he uttered, his voice still hoarse. *Can she not feel the heat? Do I help her?* Looking around, he saw no fire extinguishers or buckets of water he could use to put out the fire.

She laughed, the sound of wind chimes. "Oh, well, aren't you so sweet? It is nice to know there are young men who still know how to compliment a lady."

"Yes, you're welcome, but I mean…" he stammered. He gave a few quick nods, motioning for her to shift her attention downward, but she would not break eye contact.

Neither Juan Pedro nor Raquel commented on this woman being on fire, the flames of which had now reached her waist. Since they would be of no help, Miguel pointed at her as the words erupted from his mouth. “Your dress!”

“Hmm,” she murmured with a polite smile, not seeming to understand what he was saying, as if he had forgotten a key part of his sentence. With a slow, deliberate motion, she glanced at the floor, trying to find the source of his distress. She gave herself a once-over, turning to look behind her and even looking under her shoes, but did not appear to notice that she wore a belt of fire.

Then her face lit up in a relieved, warm laugh. She waved her hand to dismiss his concern. “Oh, *that* fire! Yes. Of course, it is still burning. You caught me in the middle of getting ready for tonight’s festival.” She wiggled a finger at him. “I see you are a naughty boy, Miguel, interrupting a lady as she gets dressed. Did you come here early to get a peek at me? How naughty! I would think you’d have known better than that.” She clicked her tongue in disappointment but otherwise seemed to consider the matter settled.

The others continued their tasks, either unimpressed or uninterested in their conversation. Raquel busied herself with checking bottles, cleaning the counter, and confirming her stock of mixed drink paraphernalia. Juan Pedro tuned his guitar on the stage, which had grown to twice its original size. Other men in matching suits had joined him, working to prepare the stage for their performance.

Miguel wanted to help the woman on fire, even if no one else seemed to care. However, as he opened his mouth to protest, he stopped. *How did she know my name?*

"Do not worry about the fire. Nothing in my home can hurt you. Relax, have a drink, and enjoy the night." There was a playful mirth to her tone, one that made Miguel smile despite everything going on around him. Cool relief flowed into his mind, merging with the last embers of panic in his stomach. Combined with his thirst and confusion, the room started spinning before him. He leaned back on the counter.

What is going on here? I know it was a one-floor shack, but now I can see it's a two-story… restaurant? Reception hall? He had to admit that his surroundings were much bigger than they had appeared from the outside. None of what he was seeing added up with the memories of his arrival. *How are they doing this? Trick walls? Mirrors? What happened to me before I came in here? Was I drunk or high? But I don't do any drugs, and I only drink with my friends. Even then, it's been a while since I've seen any of them.*

Thoughts of his friends flowed into his mind, drinks and meals shared, plans made, and trips taken. A faint smile came to his face as a stray thought floated forward. *I need to get home. They're coming over today.* The thought perplexed him. *Why were they coming over?*

"It is a lot to take in, isn't it?" the bronze-skinned woman offered, interrupting his thoughts. The crackling fire of her dress had reached her stomach now, and still she ignored it. "I'm sure you have many questions and more than a few concerns. We do not get many early visitors, so I can see how our setup could disorient someone not familiar with the behind-the-scenes of our business. Here, let me help you," she whispered, drawing his attention and meeting his eyes. "Be still."

Everything rippled like water after a stone broke the surface, and she was that center point. Little by little, the room fell away. The scent of burning dress faded from his nose, the overhead lights dimmed to specks like stars in a night sky, and the scratching in his throat vanished. Eventually, all that existed for Miguel were her steel-gray eyes.

The emerald sparks in those gray orbs flared into full flames, engulfing her irises. She blinked, and that slight disruption of eye contact jostled him from his tranquility. He let out a sigh of relief as the room stopped spinning and went still. In fact, the room was far too still. Motion was no longer an option for anyone or anything. Only she could move; only this woman seemed to truly exist. He wanted to step away, to do anything, but his body would not respond.

"I'm sorry. I'm not used to dealing with the guests one on one like this. I seem to have gone too far," the woman told him, although it sounded like she was speaking more to herself. "Please, resume enjoying yourself." A weight fell from Miguel, and sensation came back to his body. Around him, motion returned to the room.

As he enjoyed the ability to move his limbs, she stepped to within arm's reach, and that familiarity returned. Whatever memory was trying to get his attention, it never had the strength to stay long enough for him to recollect what it meant. Yet some part of him believed he knew this woman. *At least*, he puzzled, *I feel like I should. Is she a movie star? Is this a celebrity bar? It would explain the beautiful women and all the smoke-and-mirror room changes. Am I on a movie set? But how would I have gotten here? I work in an office, not on a stage or studio.* No matter how much he turned the questions over in his mind, he could find no answers.

Miguel shifted his focus to what facts he knew. *I don't know anyone famous, and I'm not famous. I am as plain as day, so if I am on a movie set, it's a mistake.* He thought about Raquel, Juan Pedro, the others in the band, and the newcomer. They dressed neatly in fine clothing. Miguel wore a simple polo, khaki pants, and brown shoes. The nicest piece of clothing he had on was a new brown belt. Compared to everyone else, he appeared underdressed. Surely his attire alone must be enough to convince them he should not be here.

“You look fine,” the woman cooed again, seeming to respond to his thoughts. She offered him her hand, and Miguel accepted it without hesitation. A comforting pulse of reassuring heat ebbed through the fabric. “Besides, if you want to change, you are always welcome to do so.” Before he could ask anything, she continued. “I am sorry you did not receive a kinder welcome. Our motto here is ‘we live to serve.’” Her eyes drifted to the others. Miguel felt himself missing her attention, even for that brief moment that she had looked away. “We pride ourselves on offering only the *best* of service here. Isn’t that right, Raquel? Juan Pedro?” Her voice boomed, though she was not shouting.

“Yes,” they replied in perfect unison.

“W-Where… Where is… here?” he muttered before breaking into a cough. “Exactly?”

She removed her hand from his, and a tingling numbness replaced the warmth it had offered. The lady in red made a sweeping, grandiose gesture around the room. As she spun in her circle, tracing the air with deft fingers, the room changed again. This time, Miguel watched the alternation. Chairs quivered in place, painted color ebbing over them, and their shapes took on a more ornate, stylized appearance. The walls became coated in a white sheen, and tablecloths popped out from the center of tables and flowed over their surfaces. Napkins, folded in intricate patterns, sprang from the tablecloths like small flowers emerging from the soil. At every table's center, an ivory candle formed. Small wax droplets flowed upward, stacking and solidifying on top of each other until a new candle had been formed. Each table's candle sparkled with a distinct color, filling the room with a rainbow of twinkling lights. With a simple wave of her hand, the room had changed from a drab bar to a radiant reception hall. Raquel's counter had even changed to match the new décor and had moved back several feet, leaving Miguel and the newcomer at the room's center.

He recognized the new layout. While the space was far larger, the layout, colors, and themes matched his and Vanessa's wedding reception. He scanned the room, seeking his wife, expecting her smiling face to appear when he turned at *just* the right angle. Vanessa would smile like she had that night when her brother played on stage and they had their first dance as a married couple. Her eyes had twinkled, and she barely managed to hold back tears and prevent messing up the makeup she had spent so long applying. Pride welled in his heart. They had made that night their own. As he finished his review of the room, his heart sank. Vanessa was not here.

The hostess's words pulled him back into the moment. "Welcome, Miguel, to my establishment, Madame MUERTOS, FORMERLY LOS CINCO HERMANAS."

If this had all been a stunt, it was the best he had ever witnessed, done with perfect timing and what should have been impossible tricks of the light. Miguel gave an appreciative clap. No one else joined him or even appeared to notice. They continued with their activities without a care or even a curious look.

“I thought we were calling it ‘Cinco Somewhere’?” Raquel gave a dry chuckle.

“As I am the headliner, it really should have *my* name in there somewhere… How else are people to know that Juan Pedro is playing the big stage? We would not want them to miss my big performances.”

“Madame… Muertos…” Miguel muttered to himself, understanding starting to seep into his mind. “So does that mean…” He stopped, shifting his gaze from person to person. He swallowed hard, not wanting to say any more, fearful that saying his thoughts aloud would make them real. “Does that mean you will kill me?”

The trio regarded him with blank expressions. Raquel put down the glass she had been shining, leaning on the bar with predatory anticipation. Juan Pedro stopped adjusting the strings of his guitar mid-motion, squinting with concern. The fiery woman winced in pain at his comment.

A knot formed in Miguel's stomach as he deduced the cause of his hazy thoughts. *They drugged me. That's why Raquel wanted me to drink more of whatever they slipped me. That is why I can't notice things changing around me, why they will not let me use the phone. They mean to kill me, but why?*

Juan Pedro and the woman on fire laughed while Raquel's glower returned to a scowl. "This guy!" Juan Pedro boomed, his face turning a bright crimson. From his coat's pocket, he produced a handkerchief embroidered with his initials in large golden letters and wiped tears from his eyes.

"No, Miha." The hostess giggled, waving her hands in a gesture meant to settle his nerves. "I can see your confusion, but no, we are not here to *kill* you. This place shares my name." With a curt bow of her head, she added, "I am, as you can guess, *the* Madame Muertos. Juan Pedro, Raquel, and I are…" She studied the others' faces for answers. "I guess you'd call us party planners."

“Party planners? In a bar named Madame Muertos. That seems a little… dark, doesn’t it? I mean, there can’t be too many parties with that theme, right? Wait, if you are party planners, why don’t you have a phone? What kind of bar doesn’t have an outside line?”

“I find it is best to think of this place as a secluded resort, not only a bar. It helps when things get… Well, when things get large.” Juan Pedro nodded with a compassionate grin.

“When they get large? You mean when the show starts? What—”

Slamming down the glass she had been cleaning, Raquel let out an exasperated snarl. “Oh for… You’re dead, you idiot.”

Chapter 3: Drinking with the Dead

"I'm… I'm… dead?" Miguel balked, disbelieving the words as he spoke them. "No… No! That can't be right, can it?" He looked from Madame Muertos to Juan Pedro. "I must not have heard her correctly, yes? I mean, that's crazy talk, right?"

Neither met his eyes, instead casting disappointed looks at Raquel. "What?" She snorted. "He would figure it out eventually, and he isn't a normal customer. Let's cut to the chase, figure out what his problem is, and get on with it. We're opening soon, and he's holding everything up."

"Raquel," Muertos warned, her sweet tone souring. "We have *talked* about this. We do not *tell* people they are dead. You *know* the problems that can cause. It is up to them to come to terms and move on. That is not our place or purpose. We are servants to the recently deceased. We guide and aide, not order and instruct. Now, what do you have to say for yourself?"

The bartender exhaled and took a step back. "Sorry you're dead," she spat before slamming another drink onto the bar for Miguel. "Drink up."

Miguel's knees grew weak. Reaching out, he found the back of a chair to prop himself up on. "I don't understand. How could this happen? I was at work this morning. I went out for lunch, like I always do. I stopped to pick up some things for my wife. In fact, I was on the phone with her, heading across the street to my car when—"

"Ah! Mi amigo," Juan Pedro chimed in, stopping Miguel from saying much more. "We find it is best not to think *too* hard on the *how* of these things, yes? It only brings sorrow and pain and makes things more difficult. Today is a cheerful occasion." He strummed his guitar. "You should celebrate."

"Celebrate? But you told me I'm dead," Miguel shouted, looking at his feet. He flexed his right hand, remembering the sensation of the plastic bag he had been carrying before he found himself outside of this bar. *I stepped out to get in the car, and*— "A car… I must have been hit when I crossed the road to get to my car. My god. Vanessa… The last thing she would have heard from me is me getting hit… the crash. She must be so worried. I need… I need a phone!" Tears streamed down his face as he met Muertos's eyes. "Please, let me use your phone. I need to talk to my wife to let her know I'm safe, that I'm okay."

Madame Muertos's eyes grew damp, but her expression remained impassive. "No."

"No? But I thought you were in customer service? I need—"

"I said *no*!" Muertos's voice boomed with thunder. Her warm appearance fell away, her body overlaid with a cold silver-blue sheen. Miguel drew back and noticed Juan Pedro and even Raquel appeared to be doing the same. Then, with a sharp exhale, Muertos calmed herself, and the silver-blue color vanished, replaced by her original bronze skin, silky black hair, and full red lips. Her tone became inviting once more, her cadence calm and pleasant. "No, you cannot use my phone." Holding up a hand, she halted any new protests from coming. "First, you are *not* okay. You are dead. For another, you are *not* safe. At least not in the way you think. While I am sorry *how* you became aware of the truth, you are now aware of your death, and the dead do not talk to the living." She paused, long enough for him to process her words but not giving him enough time to speak. "Tell me, Mr. Miguel, would it give your wife any comfort to hear from you now? For her to know you are dead and where you are now? Or would it only confuse her and everyone she told? They would think her insane from grief."

Miguel wanted to challenge her, to say something brilliant that would undo her argument. But nothing would change the fact that he was dead. Now he could only try to figure out what that meant. "So what happens to me now?"

Madame Muertos cast him a sympathetic look. She stepped forward and guided his head to her shoulder. Dazed, Miguel offered no resistance. Patting his hair in a soothing motion, she spoke in a soft whisper. "There, there, it will be all right. Everyone dies." As odd as her words were, it did give him a bit of comfort. Also, on some level, it felt familiar.

"Is this… Is this the afterlife? Am I in heaven?"

Raquel snorted, an obnoxious sound mirroring her demeanor. "Yeah, right. No one up there can pour a drink."

Miguel felt Muertos's head swivel toward Raquel. Perhaps she was debating how to best respond to the comment, but she soon returned her attention to Miguel. With slow, practiced motions, she guided him into the chair before taking the seat next to him, her back to the bar. Miguel wondered if this was to minimize distractions and suppress any desire to rebuke further comments from Raquel while they talked.

"Does that mean I'm in… in the other place? I know I was no saint, but I like to imagine I was a good man, that I helped people. That was my job. I don't think I was so bad to end up… If this is…"

"No, no, no! You are not there. You're not really *in* the afterlife right now."

"But you said… Well, *she*"—he pointed at Raquel—"said I'm dead. If I am not in the afterlife, does that mean I can go back?"

"No," Muertos replied in a still voice, placing one hand over his. "Please, listen." She cleared her throat. Her words held a nervous undertone, impressing upon him that she was telling a secret or sharing something that was not common knowledge. "Here, we offer a service to the recently deceased. A warm cup to soothe the soul from the chill of death, an icy drink to cast off the heat of life, a meal with friends and family that will fill a person with all their happiest memories. Some come for a cup of chili, others a last game with old friends, and plenty merely seek a last celebration of a life lived. Whether it was well lived or not, I cannot say."

He said nothing, staring at her as she spoke. *Why do the dead need a meal? What good are games to the deceased? How could there be a celebration of life in a place operated by death?*

"I'm sorry," Muertos replied, reading the vacant expression on his face. "Perhaps I'm not explaining this properly. You see, no one who comes here ever truly knows they are dead. Food and games are a part of life, so we use them to bring souls together, to help the dead find a connection to move on. Something familiar they can hold, at least briefly." She sighed and muttered something unintelligible. "Um, well… look at it this way. Everyone has a birthday, yes?"

He nodded, grasping that much.

"Good, good. A birthday is something they would celebrate with loved ones every year. Well, here, instead we celebrate with a Death Night Festival. A festival in honor of the night you died." She flashed him a warm smile. "Oh, and we only do it once per customer. As, you know, you only die once, yes?"

He pinched the bridge of his nose, trying to rub the building tension from his mind. "I guess so. What does that mean I'm supposed to do now?"

"At the least, you do what everyone does when they arrive: enjoy tonight. Madame Muertos is here for you. It is open to everyone who passes from the land of the living on their way to the next place. Tonight, everyone who died since last night will pass through. We receive them and celebrate the conclusion of life. Their friends and family who have come before will return here to collect them." Miguel lifted his head, a spark of hope in his eyes, but she continued before he could ask the question. "Yes, everyone will come, and they will all celebrate. Celebrate with *only* the best of food, drink, games, and music. I demand *nothing* less of my home than the best. At the night's end, everyone will move on. Where and what that destination will be, I cannot say because I do not know. Only they will know." She rose to her feet, staring into the rafters while still clutching his hand in hers.

He grinned. Her passion for this place was infectious, and he wanted to lose himself in what she said. However, Miguel kept coming back to the realization that he was, in fact, dead. He looked up at her, and she gazed down at him. Again, a pang of remembrance hit his heart. A face regarding him happily, a face so full of joy and excitement. *Who is she to me?* But the memory faded, leaving him confused. "So if that is the way things work, why am I here early? Vanessa usually kept me on time for things. Otherwise, I'd be late." He laughed, but no one else joined him.

"Is he a near-death experience?" Raquel said with concern, the glass in her hand slipping an inch before she caught it. "I hate those things. So creepy. Just… just standing out there. They don't come in. They don't move. They just… stand there." She spoke with complete disdain, shifting her gaze to the door. It was not fear in her voice, but a look of disgust mixed with incomprehension. "Why…" she whispered more to herself than anyone else.

Everyone stared at the bartender. Miguel gaped at her in confusion. Juan Pedro nearly let his guitar slip from his hands as he turned to regard Raquel. He caught the neck of his instrument, leading to an awkward twang. Madame Muertos looked on with the practice gaze of an employer who had dealt with an issue too many times already. Time crawled as they each mulled over a proper response.

Muertos broke the silence, steering the conversation back on topic. "Since you are not"—her tone changed to mimic an off-key version of Raquel's tough-girl growl—"just standing there… Ugh!" She paused, her voice resuming its uplifting tenor. "We can tell you are *not* a near-death experience. No, you see, Mr. Miguel, my home calls to all who have passed. This place is special. It plays the part of a host as much as I do. It grows to nurture the needs of those who come. There is space for all, and it will always be enough." She turned her head away, biting her lip while focusing on a dark corner of the room. "At least it is for all who accept it. This is why the house grew as we arrived for the night. Not to scare or startle you. It is only… Well, you got here early. In a way, you are seeing the show behind the curtains. But now…" There was hesitation in her voice, but also eager anticipation. A coy expression crossed her face. "Tell me, how did my home appear when you arrived?"

"Um, it's your bar. Surely you know what it looks like."

"Oh, yes," she said with a dismissive wave of her hand. "I know how it appears when I am here. It shows me what I want. However, none of us have ever seen it before we arrive to prepare for the night. I'm curious to know what you experienced, what it must have been like to be the first person in the bar before even Raquel arrived."

Miguel shook his head. "Nothing special. All I could see was a rundown old dive bar. A few tables, dusty and smelling rank. Somewhere I would have never come if not for the heat outside." His head shot up. "I'm sorry, Madame. I… I don't mean to offend."

"No offense taken. You were only answering my question. It is a little strange that it was so hollow. So empty. So worn and broken."

"You said it looked as you wanted it. Maybe it appeared as I would expect. I've always been a plain man. Nothing special about me."

Madame Muertos considered his words for a moment, then smirked. “A plain man named Miguel. There is humor in that thought, I think. No. No, there is something unique about you or else you would come in like any other patron. Like everyone else, you would have felt like you were going out to meet old friends and family, not confused and exhausted. If you are here, it means you are here for a reason. We’ll merely have to find out why by the night’s end.”

“Why do I have to have a *reason* for being here? Couldn’t I just be dead and celebrating?”

"Didn't you hear her, dingus? You were here early. No one does that." Raquel focused on the glass in her hand. A bad smudge had appeared on it and defied her every attempt to clean it. Her pace increased to a blur until she threw the rag down in defeat. She let out a long, angry breath before staring at the ceiling, reacting to an unseen and unheard speaker from above. She made a series of motions with her head, nodding, twisting, and shaking for several moments. Neither Muertos nor Juan Pedro seemed to notice and made no response to her actions. Instead, they waited, as if she were finishing a phone call. When she turned her attention back to Miguel, her voice was somber, quiet, but it carried the same serious intent as her other comments. "If you can't find a reason for moving on, you'll be a soul without a destination."

"We in the business call those souls Lost Ones," Muertos added. There was an underlying pain in her voice, something raw. "We find it helps to have something to call them."

He coughed, a panicked ache growing in his heart. "But I'm not one of the Lost Ones. You said yourself I am different from them. So why do I need to find a justification to move on? Shouldn't my being dead be reason enough?"

"A unique situation does not always mean it is better, but neither does it make it any worse. Something bigger is transpiring, a kind of game with all of us as pieces. A price will be paid. I promise you." A hardness entered her voice. "This is made all the more difficult since we only have one night to find the answer."

"Why only one night? If I cannot move on, couldn't I stay here? Try again tomorrow?"

"Closing time is still closing time." Raquel sighed. She held up the troublesome glass, gave it an approving nod, and returned to cleaning new spots that had appeared on its surface. "The bar closes at dawn, rolls back up. Literally here." The corners of her mouth turned up slightly in a wicked smile. "Everyone leaves or has already left. Some move on. Some wander the… out there, wandering with nowhere to go, never resting. Some make it back to the land of the living, haunting their old lives, existing as broken shells of their old souls. Eventually, they… stop being and fade into nothing."

"The lucky ones get to stop being," Muertos remarked, a chill weaving into her warm voice. Tension hung in the room with only the hum of the overhead lights making a sound. She gave his hand another reassuring squeeze, but who she was trying to comfort was hard to say.

"It's okay, even if I am one of these Lost Ones, you can come out and get me once you figure it out, right? I would only be outside. It's hot, sure, but I bet I could make it for a little while."

"Make it for a little while," Muertos echoed with bleak humor. "No, I am sorry, but once they are lost, there isn't much that can be done to call back the Lost Ones. We have all been trying for many, *many* years. Nothing reaches them. Even my family cannot earn their attention. You would have better luck talking to a shadow or touching a mirage. Their minds are too broken by separation from their hearts. They do not hear the here and now anymore. They merely dwell in their regret, anchored in their pain. No longer being would be a mercy to them."

"Is that right?" Raquel hissed back. "Is that how you rationalize—" Muertos cut her off with a glare, and the women's eyes locked, frozen stare meeting searing scowl.

"Some things must be done to give peace, Raquel. Sacrifices for a greater good. Of *anyone* here, I would think you would appreciate that sentiment."

"Yeah. Means, ends, all that." The bartender trailed off, returning to scrubbing the glass she had been working on with renewed vigor.

The regret in Muertos's voice brought up a pang of memory about the hostess. Something wriggling beneath the surface of Miguel's mind was telling him the answer should be obvious, but his brain refused to yield it. It was a safe, familiar memory, but not one he could recall. Muertos reminded him of *who*, exactly*?*

Returning her focus to him, she forced a smile. "We must not give up hope. You are different, Miguel. You may consider yourself a plain man, but that does not mean there is not a reason for your being here. No one comes before we open. *I* did not even think it was possible. Even Raquel had to wait for me to open the door for her."

Tears welled in Miguel's eyes. Sure, his life had not been the stuff of legend, but he had striven to be a kind person. Now he was dead and alone. Instead of a path to the afterlife, he was being told he was "special" and might not move on. No friends, no family or loved ones coming to his aid. The thought tore at his heart. *That must mean I'm first to the party. If I don't find a reason for me being here, does that mean I won't be able to greet them when their time comes? This seems like a lot of pressure to put on a simple counselor.* He tried focusing on anyone he might have lost, but no names came to him. *If this place usually prevents people from knowing they are dead, would I not know others are dead?*

A thought struck him, and he wondered how he had not considered the idea sooner. He *had* lost someone. His mother had passed soon after he was born. *Why wasn't she here?*

Pressure built in his head. The more he thought about the living and what they must be going through, or why his deceased mother was not here, the more the pain grew. Raquel set a drink in front of him, the distinct click of glass on wood drawing him from his thoughts. "Yes, it sucks, but you'll get through it. Do not worry. Comfort is on its way." She paused, again looking upward. "For everyone. I can guarantee that. Plus, humans can be a lot tougher than most of us give them credit for."

"Humans? Aren't you all spirits?"

Madame Muertos gave a somber giggle, giving Miguel the impression he had been so wrong that all she could do was laugh. "No, Raquel and I are not spirits. Juan Pedro is one who has passed. But… there was an arrangement made." Raquel rolled her eyes at the explanation. "Unlike you, however, Juan Pedro came in through the usual methods. But no, I am the hostess here. Raquel is"—she regarded the bartender, considering her words—"here to learn some valuable soft skills that she… lacked in her old job. I'll leave saying anything more to her."

Raquel offered no clarification, only a slight nod to confirm Muertos's assessment. Her focus was on the amber ale she had placed in front of Miguel. "Drink it. You'll feel better." The words fell from her mouth, sounding right but her manner not conveying the kind spirit it intended. "Trust me. I'm an expert at comforting people. I'm very relaxing."

Of all the things Miguel had heard tonight, that had to be the hardest to take in. Still, angering the scary woman, who he had just learned was not human, would probably be the stupidest thing he could do. Instead, Miguel turned his focus on the drink. "Getting drunk probably won't help."

"It's not really alcohol." Madame Muertos smiled, a little embarrassed. "You wouldn't believe how hard it is to get a liquor license. So many forms and so much legal red tape. No…" She clapped her hands, recovering some of her energetic tone. "No, what is in that glass is pure happiness."

Miguel arched an eyebrow. *Now we have a new contender for the hardest thing to believe.*

"You aren't in the physical world any longer. We make everything here to bring joy to my guests, at least for one night. It is all made to bring out the best memories the consumer has ever had. What you see, hold, taste, and experience are not just drink, food, or whatever you find pleasurable, but the happiest memory represented by what you see. Pure, joyous moments tailor-made as you remember them."

“It also keeps the Morose at bay,” Raquel offered, as if that simple term explained everything. Seeing the confusion on his face, she sighed. “Forgot how dumb humans can be. The Morose is that lost, confused feeling you are getting.” She shrugged, unimpressed by the notion. “I’ve never felt it. I *always* know what I am, where I stand, but it happens to all of you dead people. It gets you in an emotional headlock and drags you down into oblivion. It bogs the Lost Ones down. They won’t drink it themselves, so it doesn’t work on them. This drink keeps the Morose from taking hold when the celebration isn’t enough by allowing your spirit to demand its happiness back.” Her actions mirrored her analogy, and Miguel noted the satisfaction she took in her reenactment. Muertos gave Raquel a polite nod, pleased by her employee’s explanation, if not her display.

Miguel took a sip, testing it for the promised effect. His university days flickered in the front of his memories: being out with friends after a long week of lectures and assignments, moments filled with laughter and joy. As the memory finished, he set the glass down and heard himself letting out a deep, satisfied sigh on par with Juan Pedro’s reaction earlier.

With one sip, he was restored. His throat no longer ached, the sunburn no longer throbbed, and the cuts on his hand had healed. The fog covering his memories cleared. Nothing had fully formed yet, but he was becoming more of his usual self. The panic and anxiety that had churned at the bottom of his stomach dulled, strength welling up inside him. He was not drunk or even fuzzy-headed. Miguel downed the rest of the glass's contents and a wave of euphoria washed over him as memories from his university days sprang to mind. He smiled as the Morose faded away.

"You know, I'm thinking being dead isn't all bad," he replied, content for the first time since entering the bar. "I mean, sure, I don't really know who it would be, but you're saying my ancestors will come and get me? That happens here, right? I just sit back, drink, eat, and party until I get picked up?"

"Yes, but if they were coming, you'd see them already," Juan Pedro shouted from the stage. The room was now twice the size as it had been before he sat down, and the stage Juan Pedro practiced on had gone from a simple step-up to a full stage complete with curtains and stairs. "There is no one banging on the door to get in, and the door does not stick."

“Most of the time,” Madame Muertos said, drawing her arms to her shoulders for comfort. He might have imagined it, or it might have been an aftereffect of the drink, but he was sure she had shivered. Realizing he was staring at her, Muertos shook her head, sending her flat black hair twirling to distract him while she regained her composure. “You are an interesting case. I can’t recall the last time someone came here before we opened.” She cast a glance at the others, who shook their heads. “However, everyone must move on. I will have to monitor you. I don’t think you are here to bring any ill will to me and my home, but… we must be ready for the worst.”

Miguel nodded. “Thank you. For what it’s worth, I’m sorry to be a bother. I never stood out in life, and now, on my first day dead, I cause problems.”

Madame Muertos gave him a gentle smile. “That’s not true. Trust me, I am an expert on guiding life, for what it’s worth,” she said, echoing his sentiment. “Tonight, I think, will be unique even for me. You see, there is one more matter we should discuss.”

The bell on the front door, another recent change in the room, clanged as the door swung open.

Miguel tilted his head, trying to identify who was entering through the door. *Who could it be? There was no one else out there when I arrived.* Above the newcomers, the sun was setting, shining a focused beam of light directly into his eyes. For a moment, he hoped it was someone coming for him, but as the newcomers poured in, he did not recognize anyone.

Groups of people entered the bar, outlines against the blazing heat. Behind them, more people gathered outside, laughing together at a shared joke or a story's end. Miguel wondered how they could endure the heat without complaint or any sign of discomfort. A few minutes ago, he had struggled to climb the steps to the door, but all of them appeared unfazed by the temperature. In fact, it appeared they were enjoying a summer night. *Is this how it works for those who come the right way?* The recent arrivals gathered in the foyer and on the patio, both recent additions since Miguel had last looked in that direction.

For the first time since Miguel had pointed out that she was on fire, Muertos took notice of the flames on her dress. Her eyes opened wide in surprise. "Is it *that* late?" Muertos cursed. Her warm expression became a hard and tense mask.

The Death Night Festival had begun.

Chapter 4: The Opening Act

Miguel had been at restaurants and bars when they opened before. There was always an awkward greeting from the staff, the questions about if they were open or not, and finding a seat while they finished preparations. A brief time later, other people would arrive, and you were just another face in the crowd.

Madame Muertos's home had no buildup, no slow trickle of customers. Instead, they arrive en masse and flood through the front door. The entrance had split into a series of ornate double doors, each containing its own distinct Dias De Muertos motif in shades of orange, green, and purple. The opening moments were a blur of motion. "Showtime, everyone!" Muertos shouted before placing herself between the open door and the bar, alone against the surging crowds.

She is not blocking the crowd. She's greeting them.

Raquel's hand shot out, not to pour or ready drinks but to switch off the bar's backlighting. The bar's lighting went dark, with the remaining overhead lights clicking off in rapid succession. Before the stage lights went out, Juan Pedro rose from his stool to stand before his microphone. With a final nod, he and the stage fell into darkness. All of this happened over the span of seconds. The only light sources remaining were the decorative tabletop candles, which only illuminated the tables' centers, leaving the room in darkness.

Miguel gulped, savoring the last remnants of his drink. It helped his nerves but did not remove the tension in his stomach. There was a charge in the air, an energy building up and readying itself to erupt.

A whoosh of air hitting fire filled the air, and Muertos's dress flared. She became a fiery beacon in an ink-black sea. Thick plumes of smoke rushed away from her, blocking out the faint light from the candles and making them little more than embers.

Miguel heard screams of concern and shrieks of panic from the newcomers. *How must this look to them? In a strange place that suddenly goes dark, and then a woman bursts into flame and smoke. They don't even know who she is. I barely know.* He pursed his lips, wanting to call out to them, to tell them it would be okay.

As the words rise in his throat, his jumbled memories cleared for a moment. In the fog of thoughts, a memory came to mind: when he had just started his job, his first client. He met with a youthful woman, reviewing paperwork as they spoke. He said something, and the woman rose in tears and ran from the room. The door slammed behind her and jarred Miguel back into the moment. *What was it I said? I thought I was helping, but if I had said nothing, she might not have left. She would not...*

The smoke swirled and spun around the room. Miguel found it odd that he could make out the smoke against the shadows. *Is that because of the drink?* As the smoke pulled away from the tables, the candlelight went out, but the colors remained as glowing embers in the smoke, wisps of the candlelight floating upward and changing the smoke into bright, vibrant colors. Radiant energy crackled along the smoke tendrils before merging back into the surrounding darkness.

The panicked screams faded, replaced by the sounds of curiosity and bewilderment.

With a distinct pop, a single spotlight came on, shining down on Madame Muertos. All eyes were upon her as she stood alone in the only light.

Her red dress had been burned black, smoke wafting around her. She stood in silence before them, head bowed and eyes closed.

A ring of smoke swirled over her head, drifting down in an ever-thickening ring. As it touched her head, it shifted, changing from thick, sooty smoke to a black Sombrero Cordobés Con Pompón, a black, large-brimmed hat with tiny cotton balls hanging from strings. The cotton balls, or pompoms, traditionally red, were ebony black. Her face was striking. The returning smoke had painted it in the image of an ashen white skull. Large black patches covered her eyes, and slight lines etched out a toothy design of a grin over her lips. The smoke that had touched the candles settled on her in patterns of color. Small bloodred hearts dotted each cheek, with ornate black accent lines swirling around, outlining the edges of her eyes. She wore the guise of La Catrina, a goddess of death.

Miguel's mouth hung open, awed by her morbid beauty. Her appearance and demeanor were no longer warm and welcoming, instead taking on a predatory malice and hunger. Her eyes opened, earning gasps of surprise from several of the gathered souls. The green sparks that had flickered across her eyes earlier ignited, steel gray irises seared away, replaced by a deep emerald color. The last sparks leaped from her eyes and ignited the pompoms of her hat. As one pompom lit, the flame hopped to the next, igniting and moving on. When the last one crackled with fire, the flame leaped to her hat's band and a ring of green flame erupted to life. The light's intensity grew ever brighter, emerald flame shifting to orange fire and then to a deep, sultry red, the same red as her dress when they first met.

Miguel swallowed hard, trying to move away, but on some level, he knew he could do nothing to escape this moment. Silence hung in the room as Muertos raised her head and extended her arms like a magnificent bird descending on its prey. She gazed at the crowd in consideration, as if trying to select a target from among them. Although she stood on the same floor as the crowd, her presence felt elevated, adding to her predatory aura. His blood ran cold.

Muertos smiled, a pleasant and welcoming grin, and with it came some measure of relief. "Welcome, everyone," the hostess shouted in her warm tone, calling out to them like a roaring fire on a frigid winter's night. "Welcome to Madame Muertos! Come in! Come in! There is food aplenty, every dish you could ever desire! There is drink, the finest ever poured! And… there… is… music!"

Juan Pedro took his cue, and the band roared to life, filling the gigantic room with the exciting and inviting sounds of celebration. The lights flicked back on, banishing the shadows, and the crowds applauded before turning to their conversations and activities.

As time resumed its usual pace, Miguel took in the room, not surprised that it had altered its appearance. To the newcomers, this alteration would happen without their knowledge, but Miguel appeared to be the only one noticing every change.

The layout no longer mimicked his wedding reception and had grown to become an exquisite ballroom befitting a Death Night Festival. Everything about the room gave off an aura of excitement and energy, the bar itself pulsing with life. Centerpieces contained colorful flower combinations, and Miguel overheard patrons making comments about the chosen flowers. For each group, the floral ensemble brought back a happy, shared memory, sparking conversation that ignited their night.

Madame Muertos turned from the front door, her face beaming with satisfaction and pride at her performance. "Oh, how I *love* being the opening act," she purred. "I should do it more often, yes?" She beamed at Miguel, who had turned a few shades paler. "What is the matter, Miguel? Too much for you? I thought you would have liked the show."

"I… I really thought you would eat my soul." The words were out before he could stop himself, but he felt compelled to answer her.

Muertos gave a dismissive chuckle with a hint of a hungry growl. "The night is young, with so many potential outcomes."

Miguel swallowed. "What?"

She giggled and waved a hand that was now adorned in a long black glove. "I kid, I kid, Miguel. It is all part of the grand show. The Muertos welcome." She regarded the growing festivities with a smile. "I have found a little fear helps to focus attention before a warm welcome and music."

Her laugh echoed in his mind, still reminding him of someone. But the memory would not focus. Instead, he wondered, *Why do I know Death?*

Chapter 5: Mingling with the Crowd

People continued to enter, and the building continued to expand. *It's growing but not changing anymore.* Glad to have the room no longer surprising him, Miguel became uneasy with the stability. If the bar's form had stabilized, it must have meant the night was in full swing, and he needed to get started figuring out how he was going to move on.

There was so much to take in now that the festival was underway. The sounds of hundreds of conversations grew to fill the space. None of them were sad or confused. Instead, the voices carried the same level of excitement as when best friends reunited or beloved relatives made surprise visits. Miguel smiled. He could listen to their cheerful stories and excited calls all night. *It would be so easy to stand here and bask in their happiness. Lucky people like this... it's what I always wanted for my clients.*

The overhead lights, which had flared at the end of Madam Muertos's introduction, had dimmed to fit the mood of a nighttime party. People were already dancing. *That is something I wouldn't be caught dead doing. I was hopeless at my wedding. I'm sure dying hasn't made me any better.*

A loud splash caught his attention, and he turned toward the full-length windows revealing outdoor patios and various tiers containing pools of every shape and size. People were already splashing and playing in the water.

So many cheerful people and so many conversations made his head swim and his eyes blur. There was so much to see, hear, and do. *I could stay here for a while and make a plan. Enjoy the moment—*

Focus, a cool voice spoke into his mind. It was a slow, even voice, like the speaker had just finished yawning. Miguel searched for the source; whoever or whatever had spoken into his head must still be somewhere nearby. None of the gathering crowds were looking in his direction, and no one even acknowledged he was there.

You must focus, or you'll remain a blissful fool, another voice snapped into his mind. Agitated, Miguel looked around again. He had just turned when the room spun. His vision blurred, and the sounds of conversation became deafening. Each word, each exclamation, boomed in his ears. It was all too much. The emotions of the surrounding groups poured over him, and his eyes watered from the strain of processing so much all at once.

Who? What? Where am I? He staggered, falling forward on one foot.

Focus, Mr. Miguel. Please, you have got to or you'll flicker out. Please, you... a third voice, this one nervous and fast-paced, chirped into his mind. It continued speaking, but he could not hear it anymore. Miguel was losing himself in an overload of emotions and sensations. With each passing moment, more people entered and another wave of powerful emotions washed over him. The festival grew, and it was crushing Miguel under its weight.

Focus, he heard all three voices implore him at once, and he fought to follow their instructions.

Find something to stabilize yourself, he told himself. *You're always telling people to visualize a goal. Now do it.* His knees buckled, and Miguel fell onto all fours. The crowd became too much. People were moving everywhere; nothing was still enough for him to fixate on.

Changing tack, he shifted his gaze toward the front door until he found an open area. While people were still entering, no one was standing at the entrance. There were moments where space appeared beside the entrance, and so Miguel would focus his attention there.

For a moment, all was still. Miguel let out a ragged breath that ended in a harsh cough. Someone stepped into the empty area and Miguel readied himself for the barrage of sensations to return. The newcomer was a barrel-chested man who stopped to scoop up a frail older woman in a bear hug. "Mama!" The man chortled. "I haven't seen you in ages! How have you been?"

She grunted once under the weight of his hug before flexing her arms to free herself. She dropped a full foot before hugging him back with matching intensity. This time, the man grimaced. "Oh, you know," she growled. "I can't complain, Ricardo." Despite his larger size, Ricardo's feet slid from the force of her hug. She held him tight in that vise-like grapple until, apparently satisfied that she'd held him long enough, she released him. Tears filled her eyes. "Ricardo, have you been eating? Why, I can almost get my arms around you."

"Mama…" He sniffed and held back his own tears, a playful tone in his voice.

She grabbed his hand. "Come on. Everyone is waiting at the table. We have all your favorites. Don't let it get cold."

Ricardo laughed, and they disappeared into the crowd.

Miguel blinked. He had kept his attention on the mother and son, and now things were slowing back down. He rose again on shaking legs. The crowd was still there, the radiance of the guests' emotions surging all around him, but by focusing, he was no longer pulled into the whirlwind of their festivities.

Focus, like the voices said. One thing at a time. Nice and slow. Nodding to himself in reassurance, he glanced out at the crowds without resting his gaze on any one person or group. If something jumped out at him, he would lock onto it for a moment or two before forcing himself to look away. Miguel continued this practice until his heart no longer raced and his head stopped aching.

Find something familiar. Ground yourself, Miguel, he advised himself and turned toward Raquel's bar. While he didn't know the bartender very well, he at least recognized her and needed the comfort of that partial familiarity. A row of soldiers dressed in a variety of uniforms and ranks held glasses at the ready, all eyes on a young woman as she made a comment and started raising her glass. Miguel noticed a distinct familial resemblance among them. The young woman finished her comment, and the others roared in approval. *Best not to listen in. I might hear too much and end up on the floor again.*

Behind the bar, Raquel added something to the conversation. She made a grand gesture with her arms and raised her own drink. They all laughed, and the young woman's face turned a bright scarlet and the lineage of soldiers clinked glasses and consumed their drinks. The men in older uniforms slammed their shot glasses on the counter, exclaimed their approval, and patted the newest member on the back in congratulations. Then, called away by some unseen figure, they collected their hats from the counter, tucked them under their arms, and stepped away. Miguel noticed that a bottle had appeared in each person's hands, where none had been present a moment earlier. Together, they walked around a corner and disappeared from Miguel's sight.

Fixating on Raquel, he wondered if what he had seen was true. *Did Raquel smile, or am I still dizzy?* He risked another glance at her and found, to his dismay, that she was glaring at him.

"Hey," she said in a calm and plain tone. Despite the crowd, Miguel heard her as if they were the only ones in the room. Unlike the voices in his head earlier, Raquel's voice nullified all other sounds. It was unnerving, but at least it differed from the other intrusions to his thoughts.

Good to know there are alternatives to the voices in my head. He sighed. *Dead and crazy. Such a winning combination.*

"You tell anyone…" Raquel trailed off, leaving the threat unsaid, but she held Miguel's attention until he nodded his understanding.

When she looked away, Miguel started forward, eager to leave under his own power before she threw him somewhere. He stopped and turned in another direction, then spun again in a confused series of motions, as he found he could not commit to any one direction. *So… where should I go? Where do I want to go?*

To his right was the front door, now a pair of glass doors with golden trim. Velvet ropes and vibrant, leafy plants highlighted the path into the foyer. People entered and made their way to their personal celebrations with an unerring sense of confidence.

On the left was Raquel's bar. He did his best not to look in that direction, but he could tell that it had changed, too, growing and becoming a marble countertop with trim to match the front door. Designs in the marble matched the skull motif adorning both Muertos's and Raquel's faces.

The bulk of the room comprised tables filled with patrons, a sea of celebrating parties. At first, he had only seen random families and groups scattered around the room. There had been no rhyme or reason to any of it. But as he took this moment to study the swaying scene, he noticed an organization to the tables. He noticed that the tables were organized by meal selection. It reminded him of being in a market, with each style and type of food in its own aisle. Every row radiated from a central point on the wall perpendicular to where Miguel stood, and at the center of that wall was a set of doors he assumed led into the kitchen. Having no skill in cooking, managing a sandwich on his best days, Miguel stayed as far from there as possible. Creating a kitchen fire here might end up sending him to the afterlife's hotter side.

Before he could continue taking in his surroundings, something stopped him, an eerie sensation of someone watching him. He searched the room, but no one was looking at him. Everyone focused on their own celebrations. Still, he could not shake the sensation that there were eyes upon him, that someone or something was focusing on him. Scanning the crowd, he spotted a silver-blue sheen a few times, but it faded away before he could focus on it. The glow's size and shape varied, and it hid behind the crowds or ducked into shadows with a nimble quickness. His stomach lurched, his pulsed quickened, and a desire to run crept into his mind. *Stay calm. Stay focused*, he told himself. *Nothing can hurt you, right? You're already dead.* Taking a drawn-out breath, he blinked repeatedly to focus his vision. He scanned the floor again, no longer able to locate any silver-blue auras. *There, nothing but spots in my eyes. I probably just stared into the spotlights too many times. Or it could be the aftereffects of my dizzy spell.*

Across from the door, easily seen from each table thanks to this place, was the stage. Juan Pedro and his band performed loudly and with passion. They moved between sets and styles with the same ease as though they were breathing. A patron found her way to the stage, and the band took it in stride, laughing and allowing the amateur performer her moment in the spotlight. An instrument for the guest to play was always *just* off stage, just out of sight, and all the band members had to do was reach back for it.

Two sets of doors were to the right of the stage. The first led to the pool, which Miguel found strange, as the stage now resided both inside and outside, allowing people in any location to enjoy the music. The latter doors were large and plush, with the words *Rec Rooms* written in neon overhead. Neon letters reading *VLA* flickered above. With no swimsuit, no group to sit with, and having no desire to dance, he decided it would be best to check out the back area.

No sooner had he started forward than he stopped again. A group stepped into his path. Bracing himself for impact, Miguel winced, but the blow never came. Instead, there was a tingle as the closest person passed through the space where he was standing—or, rather, stepped through Miguel without slowing. He was uninjured, not even jostled by the dancers; it was as though he had not been there or had not even existed. His body tingled with pins and needles where he would have touched the other patrons .

"I really am a ghost."

"No, you're just not needed in their Death Night Festival," Madame Muertos replied, appearing behind him. Miguel jumped, but not as much as he had the first time. The wicked smirk on her face showed how much she had enjoyed his reaction. All things considered, her abrupt appearances made sense; death snuck up on you.

He touched his hands together, if for no other reason than the comfort of being assured he was solid. Standing next to her, he felt compelled to speak, to hold her attention. Plus, he had always hated awkward silences.

His hostess explained, “Everyone has what they need to celebrate. My home provides what they desire.”

“Are you saying people can create anything here? Could I just create a reason to move on? It’s what I need.”

She gave him a nasal laugh but shook her head. “No, nothing like that. My home can provide food, drink, and games. Things, but not purposes or memories. It can put you in your best state, as required for a Death Night Festival. Think of it as a costume party where everyone comes in their best. Young or old, at their best or worst, it is up to them how people appear. A grandmother might be an old woman when meeting a grandchild but a young señorita when she meets her love again.”

“This is unlike any Dia De Muertos festival I have ever been to. There is so, so much here. I mean, it’s people from everywhere on Earth.”

"Yes, well, that is because you're not attending a Dia De Muertos festival. This is a *Death Night Festival*, remember?" She stared out at the crowds, a longing ache in her burning green eyes. "Here things are… more complicated, more encompassing. Times change, even here." There was a finality in her statements, pain hidden under a mask of professionalism. "Unlike what my family may think," she spat, "my home adapts with the times. Sometimes that means making the hard choices, leaving past traditions behind. No matter what happens, people will still die. Someone has to be here for the departed. Tonight, they meet with their past honor and savor it one last time." There was an unsettling hint to her words, something predatory and eager to feed, a glint of silver-blue shining beneath her fiery green eyes.

It reminded him of her opening act, when he imagined she would descend upon the crowd, and tried to change the subject. "You could have warned me," he blurted, "that I would pass through people."

"You would have figured it out soon enough, I'm sure. Besides, I try to minimize how much I impact my guests. I am merely the host, not their master."

"But wasn't it one of you who helped me focus earlier? I heard a voice in my head. Well, voices, really. Wasn't that you and Raquel?"

Madame Muertos took a moment to examine him before casting a glance over her shoulder at the bartender. Raquel shrugged, shaking her head. "That was not either of us." She regarded him, an impish smile playing at the corner of her mouth. "Tell me… do you *often* hear voices, Miguel?"

"No." He shook his hands to dismiss the idea. "I… It was like someone was telling me to focus on the moment or I would lose myself."

Muertos bobbed her head, acknowledging his words. "Excellent advice. If you are hearing voices, at least they are not leading you astray."

Miguel nodded but said nothing.

Muertos gave him a measured smile. "While it has been enjoyable talking with you, and the night is young, I believe you were in the middle of something? Unless you want to stay with *me* all night." Her eyes shone with the same hunger he had seen at the night's beginning, as though she were a predator sizing up potential prey. Unlike the last encounter, his legs found their strength, and this time, he started backing away. There was an unsettling aura about her, and Miguel felt a strong need to flee.

"Ah, yes… I'll…" Miguel pointed away from her, walking in that direction. "I'll just be off. Perhaps I will see you, um, around?"

Tilting her head to one side, the hostess said nothing.

Coughing into his hand, Miguel stammered, incapable of remaining silent, "I mean, yes. Yes, I will see you. It is your home. I'll find somewhere to make myself busy and let you get back to work. I—" Miguel stopped, falling backward. His foot had struck something, and now he toppled over. His arms flailed, seeking any purchase but finding none.

He landed with a thump, not the thud he expected. Whatever he had fallen into was semi-solid and made a plopping sound. All around him, there were gasps and spurts of surprised laughter.

“Whoa,” a deep, masculine voice boomed. A few weak laughs and surprised gasps followed. Figures rose around him, reaching out to help him to his feet. Two men stood him up, their expressions a mix of concern and barely repressed amusement. His back felt wet and sticky, and Miguel hoped it was only food. “We asked for a cake topper, but this seems a little extreme,” the voice teased as rough hands knocked chunks of frosting and cake from his clothes.

Miguel turned to the speaker, craning his neck to meet the man’s eyes. This had to be the biggest man Miguel had ever seen. He had the physique of a professional bodybuilder, but he wore a svelte business suit that fit his massive frame.

“If you wanted some cake, my friend, you only had to ask.” The enormous man’s eyes twinkled with mirth.

Miguel smiled. Rubbing his back, he found his hand covered in frosting. Giving his finger a quick lick, he nodded. “Vanilla. I’m more of a strawberry person.”

The table's guests laughed, a welcoming sound, although some sounded more like they were being polite rather than expressing genuine amusement. The sizeable man wiped a tear from his eye and extended a massive hand to Miguel. "I am Hector."

"Miguel," he responded, accepting the firm handshake that lifted him off his feet. As he released Hector's hand, Miguel's arm continued the motion for a second longer. "I'm sorry to have ruined your cake. Please, let me get you another—"

As soon as the words left his mouth, a replacement seemed to materialize at the table's center. The ruined cake and surrounding mess disappeared bit by bit. In the blink of an eye, all evidence of the mess had disappeared. However, his frosted backside reminded Miguel that the accident had occurred. No one at the table moved or reacted to the vanishing remnants of their cake, as their attention was on Hector as he spoke with Miguel. *We are the center of the discussion. The only thing that matters for their festival.* Miguel paused, flexing his sore hand. *Wait, does that mean my falling into a cake was part of their plan? Did the night really want me to be a cake topper?* The image of himself falling onto the cake came to his mind, and he blushed.

But he had noticed something else as the cake disappeared. Something strange, even by tonight's standards. For a fraction of a second, Miguel swore he had seen the outline of three women setting down the fresh cake and removing the destroyed remnants. They moved in a flurry of violet, blue, and green.

"No harm done," Hector boomed. "We always have too much cake, and besides, you saved us from singing 'Happy Birthday.' None of us could carry a tune."

"Speak for yourself," a woman with a sharp accent snapped back. "Some of *us* are the definition of grace and blessed with an angel's tongue."

"Do you keep it in your purse, Auntie?" the man beside her quipped as he returned to his seat. He wiped his hands on his napkin without looking before setting it aside. Miguel watched it disappear, replaced by a fresh linen less than a blink later.

"Take a seat," Hector offered, pulling a chair up for Miguel. "We were about to cut the cake, and the more the merrier."

"No, I shouldn't intrude."

"Nonsense," a skinny older man offered with a laugh. "We already shared one cake together. What's another slice?"

Amused, Miguel sighed and took a seat, but not before laying a napkin on the chair to prevent making another mess. *One slice of cake, then I can get cleaned up.* He frowned. *Are there bathrooms here? Would that be a part of the celebration?*

"So whose birthday are we celebrating?" he asked the table. Everyone was dressed in fine clothing, but there was nothing unique to identify who the party was for.

Hector chuckled. "Oh, no one in particular. We have always got together for birthdays, but I haven't been around for a while because…" He paused, his eyes searching for an answer.

Miguel recognized the look coming over Hector's face. It mirrored how he imagined he must have looked when he tried to figure out how he had arrived at Madam Muertos's home. Juan Pedro's words echoed in his mind. *We find it is best not to think too hard on the* how *of these things, yes? It only brings sorrow and pain. Today is a cheerful occasion.*

"You were traveling?" Miguel offered, taking a sip of water to appear casual. It gave him the same euphoria as the amber liquid Raquel had provided, which helped calm his nerves.

“Yes,” Hector added after considering Miguel’s words. “Yes, that’s it. I’ve been out of town for a long time. Now we can get together to celebrate everyone’s birthday.”

The others nodded, and Miguel regarded them. Were they the genuine souls of his family or made up by the house to help Hector celebrate? Did the dead spend eternity coming back to gather those left behind? *Heavy thinking to have over cake*, he told himself as he accepted a slice. “Happy birthday, Hector,” he offered.

“Happy birthday, Miguel,” Hector echoed, handing out slices of cake to the others at the table. Miguel nodded in thanks as he took a bite of the cake.

Strawberry cream. He smiled. Miguel watched the others as they ate and talked. Auntie Geraldine, the woman with the angelic singing voice, and Fernando, the man who had helped Miguel off the cake, continued to banter back and forth, the others adding just enough to keep the conversation and laughter going. For his comments, Fernando received several hits to his arm from Geraldine, but he laughed them off and followed up with another comment.

Miguel wished his own family were here but found he could not remember the last time they had all gathered. *Usually it was only Dad and me. There never seemed to be enough time.*

A pang of sadness tugged at his heart as he wondered how things could have been different. *Maybe if Mom was there...* While he had seen pictures of his mother, Miguel had only one mental image of her. It was a fraction of a memory, and he was never sure if he had made it up or if it had even happened. That he remembered it with such clarity always made it seem real. They were still in the hospital; he could not have been more than an hour born. Exhausted, his mother lay back in her bed, her hair a wild mess, breathing in weak, tiny gasps. Despite it all, a smile spread across her exhausted face. Her arms were reaching out for him, to take him from his father, to hold him for even a moment. When he passed into her arms, a line of heat washed through his body, like he was being wrapped in another blanket. She whispered something to him, but as a baby, he did not understand what it was, and the words did not register. He was told that she had died from complications soon after. Miguel had that one moment with his mother, but he held that memory, real or not, in his mind.

He took a large bite of cake, letting the sugary sweetness distract him from the direction his thoughts were taking him. *Once I finish here tonight, I could ask Mother if that happened. If I can move on…*

"Well, this was lovely, but I think it's time we go back to my place," Fernando offered. Cheers of agreement came from the others, forks clinked onto plates, and the family rose from the table.

Hector clapped Miguel on the shoulder, jarring him from his thoughts. "Thank you for joining us, my friend. It was good you stopped by. The party needed something to get us all talking. We are hopeless at small talk."

"What?" Miguel mumbled through a mouthful of cake. "Going already? The night is still so young. Why not stay for a drink, or…?"

"Sorry, Miguel. We just stopped for cake. Now we're going back to Fernando's. I hope we'll see you around, yes?" Hector extended one of his enormous hands, and Miguel took it. "I hope you have a wonderful rest of your night."

"Yeah," he replied, wishing he had something important to say. He stumbled into their lives, or into their afterlives, and now they were leaving.

Hector released his hand, smiled his broad, toothy smile, and joined his family, who were already near the front door. With each step, Hector's group faded a little more until they vanished.

A thought came to Miguel, and he shot to his feet, racing after Hector. *Perhaps I can follow. I celebrated, so now I should be able to move on.* Hector was the last in his crowd, walking with lumbering steps toward the exit. Miguel closed the distance between them in a few seconds and reached out for Hector's hand.

Miguel's hand passed through the larger man, as the crowd had passed through him earlier. Hector turned ever so slightly while still talking to his family, but he continued to fade away, leaving Miguel alone in the foyer. He trudged back to his chair, considering the cake before shoving it away. He no longer had a taste for sweets; his mouth had gone sour. *Why didn't that work? I celebrated, right? Shouldn't that be enough?*

Frustrated, he rose, his back making a peeling sound as his clothes pulled from the chair. *Oh yeah, I'm covered in cake, too.*

"Oh, you poor dear," Muertos's voice called out as she appeared beside him. "Come, let's get you cleaned up." She led him away from the tables, as one would a child who had muddied his Sunday best.

"I don't understand. What happened? Why couldn't I move on?"

"I told you. You were not a part of their celebration. For one wonderful moment, you joined in their fun, but it could not last forever. A party is like life—it lasts only so long."

Miguel looked around, careful not to let his gaze rest on any events for too long. There were gatherings starting and ending all around them. Some were a quick cup of coffee before moving on. In other groups, one person stood at the center of a circle of people, telling stories with updates on his life and adventures.

No one is coming to help me. Out of the corner of his eye, the silver-blue images returned, flittering in and out of focus. They were not moving any closer, just circling and waiting. *But what are they waiting for?* He looked at Muertos, who gave no sign of noticing the glowing things. *What are those things? Does she not see them? What do they want with me?*

Chapter 6: Running Afoul of Raquel

Muertos and Miguel arrived at Raquel's counter, receiving the usual kind and welcoming grace only the bartender could muster. "What happened to him?" Raquel snarled. "Don't tell me we have pools filled with cake now."

Raquel's appearance had changed. She now wore a simple black corset, which seemed natural on her, almost as if her earlier attire had hindered her movements. Following Muertos's style, she had painted her face in the La Catrina style, but without the ornate lines or decorative flares. All that broke the monotony of her black and white face paint were three red lines on each cheek that angled upward to her ears and a stylized set of open wings.

"Cake pools would be available if a guest requested it," Muertos snapped back. "No, Miguel here"—she dragged him between her and Raquel—"*fell* onto someone's table and onto their cake."

The bartender paused, raising a skeptical eyebrow. "On someone *else's* table?" she repeated. "How does that happen?"

"It appears he *tripped*," Muertos replied, accenting the last word. "For now, I need you to get him cleaned up."

“What am I, his maid?”

“Really, I’m fine. I just need to wash up. If it is about ruining the cake—”

“No,” Muertos interrupted. “No, everything is… *fine*, Miguel. It’s just an old… problem between friends. Nothing that cannot be resolved quickly enough, right, Raquel?”

Raquel met Muertos’s eyes, exhaling her frustration before turning away. “Sure,” she growled. Tossing her cleaning rag to the counter, she turned her glare to Miguel. “We’re all here to help, right?”

“Good,” Muertos replied through clenched teeth. “I can always count on you for a generous spirit and to handle house matters. See to things while I continue my hosting duties. I would hate to have to deal with another staffing issue.” Without another word, she turned, and within a few steps, she vanished among the crowd.

“Hosting duties.” Raquel chuckled in a bit of dark humor. “Walking around like a Big Mart greeter. Leave me to clean up and do all the work.”

Miguel looked back at the crowds, in part to give Raquel a moment to grumble to herself but more to find Muertos in the crowd or identify those silver-blue things from earlier. When the rumbling of Raquel's words had subsided, he returned his attention to her while putting on his friendliest *don't hit me please* smile. "Do you know where I can get cleaned up? Maybe a fresh set of clothes and a place to change?"

"No changing rooms here, and no change of clothes," she snapped back before picking up her towel again to clean the glass in her hand. "You can have anything you need for your night. You know that much, right? So just be clean."

"Um… Just 'be clean'?" he repeated.

"Yes," she added, irritated. Raquel said nothing else for several minutes, focusing instead on cleaning her glass. After a few wipes, she glanced up, seeing Miguel still staring at her. She made a deflating sound, shaking her head. "Mortals…" Straightening up to her full height, which somehow made her seem more intense, she glowered. "Think of clothes like food."

“Clothes like food?” he echoed, a little sarcasm, and more than a little annoyance, creeping into his voice. “Don’t I have *enough* food on my clothes?”

“This is all in your head. Everything here…” She pointed with her glass at their surroundings. “Everything you see is what you want to see. If you think you are drinking alcohol or falling in a pool of cake, you’re doing it here.”

“So…”

“So if you think you’re clean, you’ll be clean. Muertos told you about the *if it’s needed for a celebration* aspect of this place, right?”

“So just think the mess away?” he asked. Closing his eyes, he tried to imagine what he had looked like before falling on the table, visualizing his clothes. With the image in mind, he willed away the messy clothing.

“Huh,” Raquel clucked with wry humor. “Well, you are clean…”

Miguel gasped as he looked himself over. There he stood, in the middle of a crowded bar filled with more people than he had ever seen, naked. His brain could not prioritize being terrified, mortified, or embarrassed. So it split the difference and did all three at once.

With a gasp, he tried to hide his shame. However, no matter how much he twisted and covered himself, it only made him stick out even more. Plus, he could have sworn he heard someone whistle at some point.

Can this get any worse?

"Oh, calm down." Raquel sighed. With a flourish, her arm shot out, and she snapped her fingers in his direction. Clothes, as clean and pressed as when he'd first bought them, appeared on his body. "You were naked, not on fire."

"That is oddly specific," he commented, examining himself to be sure the clothes covered *everything*.

"I've seen it happen. People let their imaginations run too wild."

"Well, I appreciate your help."

“Speaking of appreciating.” Raquel placed two fingers in her mouth and produced an ear-piercing whistle, the force pushing Miguel back and making his ears ring.

Can you be dead and have tinnitus?

At first, nothing seemed to happen. Besides Miguel, there had been no motion or disruption of the crowd to show that anyone had heard the call. The pressure in the air dropped, creating a vacuum in that air. A trio of women appeared between Miguel and Raquel’s counter, filling that sudden emptiness. Faces painted akin to Raquel’s and Madame Muertos’s, they wore white tops with colorful skirts of green, violet, and purple. The colors sparked recognition in his mind. *The women from the table? They were real!*

“What?” three female voices chimed, not quite in harmony.

“Miguel.” Glowering, Raquel pointed her glass to the newcomers. “Meet Muertos’s minions: Violeta, Azul, and Lima. The Maria trio. Wait staff for all the bar’s quadrants and rec room operators.”

"A quadrant would mean four," Violeta corrected, holding up a defiant hand with the correct number of fingers. She waved her pinky, which was her fourth raised digit. "But with only three of us, it's been busy. Can we go now, or did you only call us to show off your math skills?"

"D-d-don't fight," Lima stuttered. "We need to get back to work. We are falling behind. Oh…" She started spinning in place to look back toward the rec rooms. "Oh, I'm being called. I need… I need to g-g-go."

"I kind of enjoy the break. We get to talk to the recent arrival." Azul turned to him, rolling her neck. "Hi, Mr. Miguel. How are you liking the bar?"

"Can it, Azul," Raquel barked. "This isn't a break. You'll be getting back to work in a minute. Right now, I'm asking you something."

"Oh," Violeta Maria challenged, her voice rising and lowering in mocking octaves. "Such anger, such fire. You know that's why you're called *Raquel del Fuego*."

Unperturbed, Raquel tilted her head and snarled, "Really? I thought it was because I was the only one who looked good in red, Violeta Maria. On you, it just shows off your sausage shape."

Furious, Violeta lunged forward. Lima and Azul grabbed their sister's arms, reacting with lightning quickness while remaining distracted by their activities. To Miguel, it appeared to be a well-practiced reaction, and he wondered how often the two women had to stop their sister from attacking Raquel.

"What? Did I hit a nerve?" Raquel's voice smoldered with building anger. "Gee, I'm sorry." Her tone crackled sarcastically. "Imagine having your night ruined by someone. Like… maybe someone smashing your cake."

"That wasn't me," Violeta pouted, pulling her arms free from her counterparts. Her explosive anger had disappeared as quickly as it arose, and she returned to her normal, agitated state. "It was this guy here. He—"

He shrank back as the violet-dressed woman pointed a thumb at him.

“Miguel fell on a cake, sure,” Raquel barked out in agreement, catching Violeta off guard. Apparently, the duo did not agree on much. “But *who* set the cake right at the table’s edge when it’s normally set in the center of the table?”

Violeta blinked three times in rapid succession. “Well, I did, but I—”

“You,” Raquel growled, pointing her glass at each Maria, one after the other, “and your sisters have been hanging around up here all night, checking out the new guy when you’re supposed to be at your stations. You’re all lucky it was just a cake that got messed up and that Miguel handled the situation before we had some patrons go Morose.”

“It was only a minor mistake, nothing that could cause any actual harm,” Violeta snapped back.

Raquel’s voice went cold. “It only takes a moment of doubt for the Morose to take effect. You *know* that, right? None of them…” She held her glass forward with the same intensity as if she were holding a sword. “None of *us* are immune.” Raquel shrugged. “None of you, anyway. Remember, I don’t doubt. I know, and what I know is always factual.”

Violeta made to reply but swallowed it down. "Well—"

"We didn't mean any harm," Azul whined, stretching tired limbs. The motion also helped her avoid Raquel's gaze.

Lima was on the verge of tears. She continued to turn between Raquel and something happening far away that only she could hear. Her hand came up, and she bit her nails without noticing. Miguel wondered if she would have fingers left as her teeth chattered against her nails. "Is Chef mad that we messed up the cake?"

"Ask Chef. *After* your shift. For now, we have something else to talk about." Raquel glowered at them. "Right now," she said, stressing the words, "I need you all to get your heads out of your asses and into the game. Get back to doing your jobs." Violeta gave a sharp inhale, Lima whimpered, and Azul moaned in protest. "If Muertos saw you slacking, you know what happens?"

I should say something, try to explain. Raquel cast him a glare, and his lips tightened. *How* does *she do that with just a look?*

"We were only trying to help," Violeta Maria protested. There was a sheen to her eyes, the start of angry tears only held back by the force of her will alone. "He was losing himself in the crowds by taking in too much. He'd burn out that fool brain of his if he tried to see everything all at once and he wasn't ready." She threw a thumb in Miguel's direction, although there was none of her earlier energy behind it. "He was definitely not ready."

"I'm sorry I whistled. I thought he was trying to do something sexy," Lima whimpered, tears falling from each eye. "Please don't tell Muertos. I only wanted to make him smile." Azul reached over and patted her sister's shoulder, then leaned on her. Miguel wondered if she meant to be supportive of Lima or if it was Azul looking for somewhere to rest her head.

"It's okay. I bet he didn't even hear it." Azul stretched.

“Look,” Raquel responded with what Miguel thought must be her most civil tongue. At least civil by Raquel’s standards. “I know you’re all excited. You love having people here. It’s what you do. I also know you think you’re helping, *but…*” She paused, meeting each of them in the eyes one by one. “The point is, he is not a toy. He’s a guest like everyone else. He’s only got a little time before he’s lost forever.” Miguel shrank from her words. The reminder of his impending fate was not helping his confidence. “Don’t go hassling him or trying to get him to do your work. He’s still a guest, even if he can interact with other tables. You all know the rules. You *know* what happens if you mess up. It’s not only the guests who eat here. We clear?”

The trio hung their heads in defeat, with even Violeta no longer eager to continue fighting. In the same near unison as when they had arrived, they gave Raquel understanding hums of agreement.

"Good. We can tell Muertos it was all a simple mistake later." She paused, letting the words sink in, then snapped her fingers, jarring the trio from their thoughts, "Well? What are you standing around for? Put your party faces on and get back to work. We have guests who need to celebrate."

In a blink, the Maria trio vanished, a rush of wind pulling Miguel a few steps from the bar as they hurried back to their work.

Brushing himself off and checking to make sure their sudden departure had not been enough to pull the clothes off him again, he stepped back to the bar, out of the way of any passing crowds. Falling into one group had been enough. He did not want to risk being pulled into another party again so soon. The bar had changed so much since he first arrived. No longer a roughhewn board of untreated wood, it was now a beautiful white marble countertop gleaming with shining gold trim. Overhead, polished wine glasses refracted the light in a rainbow of illumination. "Don't you think you were a little hard on them? I mean, it was just some harmless whistling, a mess with a cake. Nothing major, right?"

Raquel turned her glare upon him, and he found that it was as bad as he feared. “I do what I have to, not because I enjoy doing it. They are staff, the same as anyone else. Focus on your work or you’re gone.”

“They were curious,” Miguel countered, although he did not put much force into his argument.

“If they want to see you, they can wait until you go to the rec rooms. If you even end up there. If not, they miss out and you move on. Probably.”

Her continuous reminders of his pending fate grated his nerves. “What’s the harm in them having a little fun?” he muttered. “Isn’t that why we’re all here?”

Something in Raquel’s eyes broke. It was not anything physical, but Miguel could see a change in her iron gaze and was certain the room’s temperature dropped a few degrees. “Are you saying I’m not fun? I will have you know, Miguel, I’m plenty of fun to be around. All of my friends would back me up.”

“I didn’t mean…” he stammered, taking a reflexive step backward. “It’s just… Well…”

As she opened her mouth to speak, she stopped, her lips becoming a hard line as her eyes fell back to the counter. Without a word, she returned to her cleaning, but she lacked her usual powerful confidence. Her appearance was still flawless, but she appeared diminished. Her demeanor was smaller, more withdrawn, as if her fiery passion had died down to a flicker.

Guilt hit Miguel square in the stomach. *What did I do?*

Raquel's words from earlier in the night whispered into his mind. *The Morose is that lost, confused feeling. I've never felt it. I* always *know what I am doing, but it happens to all you dead people. It gets you in an emotional headlock and drags you down into oblivion.*

Did I make Raquel question herself? Did I give her the Morose? He tapped the counter, testing her response like it was a frozen pond's surface. Her eyes darted toward the motion, then back to her work. They stood without speaking.

"Raquel," he offered. She grunted a quiet acknowledgment but said nothing. "I'm sorry."

Still she made no response.

"I shouldn't have made it sound like you're not fun. I'm sure you're lots of fun to be around. I've known you for a short time, is all."

Her shoulders seemed to give a slight shrug, but it was hard to make out due to how little… *I said the wrong thing again.* He remembered the woman left his office in tears.

"It's fine," she offered in a whisper, sounding mechanical and detached from the moment.

"No, it is not fine," Miguel replied. "I shouldn't have been so dismissive to a friend."

"I do my job. Let the Marias take care of entertaining. You should go see them. They are much more entertaining."

"Maybe later," Miguel said, sitting at the counter. Resting his hand on his face, he watched her clean in silence. For a few minutes, they remained quiet, Raquel twirling the glass in her hand over and over until it looked clean, then repeating the motion as new spots appeared on its surface. Miguel gave a slight cough, and she peered at him. "If I may ask, what is so special about that glass?"

Confused, Raquel lifted her head and cocked an eyebrow at the question. She regarded him, perhaps expecting a joke at her expense or something sinister. "What? This one?" She held the glass forward.

Miguel nodded. "Yes. You've been cleaning it all night. I imagine it must be special."

She regarded the tall glass, admiring how the light glistened on its pristine surface. How it cast tiny rainbows of light all around her. Then she tossed it behind her and into a bin. The sound of breaking glass echoed inside. "Nothing. It's glass, like any one of a thousand others we have here. Why do you…" She paused, realization dawning on her face, bringing back some of her usual sneer. "Wait. Do you… Do you think I've been cleaning one glass all night?" She trembled, a small shake on her lean frame. The shaking grew until it came out with a word. "Humans." She laughed. "I forget how little you see. I haven't been cleaning *a* glass all night. I've been cleaning *all* the glasses. At least, I'm cleaning when I'm not serving drinks."

As she returned to her usual abrasive self, Miguel asked questions. "But I haven't seen you leave the bar. The only times I've seen you pouring anything were for Juan Pedro and those soldiers."

"That's because I move fast." She beamed with self-satisfaction, and the old Raquel grit peeked through her grim expression. With a minor change to her uniform, she straightened to her full height. "Top of my battalion in speed and combat navigation."

"Battalion? Were you a soldier?"

"The best kind," she replied with a genuine smile on her lips, one not hidden under a scowl or smirk. "I helped save many people." For a moment, she stared up at the ceiling, a wistful gleam in her eyes. Miguel followed her gaze but could see nothing unusual.

"Is there something up there?"

Raquel chuckled, the smile lines breaking on her dour face. "There is. It's home." After a few more seconds, she shook her head, coming back to the moment. "You don't hear it? I forget how basic human hearing can be."

"You keep calling me a human, so what does that make you? You said you aren't a spirit. What else is there?"

“I am… I was an angel,” she said, letting her gaze drift around the bar to avoid looking at him.

He laughed. “You’re an angel? But why would an angel be working in a bar?”

“Isn’t anyone working service an angel?” She chuckled. “Besides, Muertos told you already. I needed to work on my ‘soft skills,’ whatever those are. Order of Raphael dedicated to healing and shelter. We are experts in comfort. That’s why I’m so good at it.”

“Comfort?”

Raquel held up a glass.

“So you served drinks in heaven?”

"No need up there," she said, stretching her neck. "Heaven has the pure source all over. You just reach out with your cup, and you got a drink of whatever you want. The job is simple up there." She looked at the ceiling. "Anyone could do it." A mean smirk followed her comment. She returned her gaze to the counter, looking displeased. There was nothing to chop or clean, and that seemed to disagree with her mood. "The house here connects into that on some level only nerds understand." She patted the series of taps before her. "These let me access it and distill it for patrons. I guard it all night, only leaving to deliver drinks."

"I thought the Marias delivered drinks?"

With a gruff snort, she shook her head. "There is no way I let them touch my drinks, much less ever let them behind the bar. Violeta has been trying for a long time to get a sample of the pure stuff. They handle special orders for the kitchen and party appearances as needed. I try to keep them in the back rooms so they can focus. Not that anyone appreciates what I do."

"I'm sure they would, but since they are in the rec rooms, they don't get the opportunity to see what you do. Like me, I haven't seen you leave the counter since the night started."

With a wry smile, she leaned against the bar. “Alright, I’ll show you. Maybe they’ll listen to you when you tell them.” She pointed out at the crowd. “See that guy drinking the mojito? Table 06-18?”

Miguel turned and squinted. There were no visible markers, so he had no idea what marked one table different than any other, but he found the man she had indicated far in the distance. He was a skinny man in a tweed suit and had just sipped the last of his drink and was lowering it to the table. “Yes, but—”

Raquel’s hand fell hard on his shoulder, almost shoving him to the floor. He jumped as she appeared beside him. Miguel tried to move away, but he was too slow, every motion responding like he was moving through thick mud. Time appeared to have stopped, yet he could still feel the momentum of his foot trying to move backward. His joints ached to move but the absence of time held him in place.

“You’re in my time now. My speed. Watch and learn. Well, watch me fly.” Raquel’s hand came off his shoulder, and she rocketed away from him. She was not running but glided through the crowd like a professional dancer, each movement graceful and with deliberate purpose. Each footfall clicked, counting out the forgotten seconds. The more she moved, the more the intense red aura pulsed around her, her feet shimmering and buzzing with power.

Raquel del Fuego. Miguel recalled Violeta’s nickname for the bartender. *Raquel of the Fire. Violeta wasn’t just making a jab at Raquel’s temper but referring to how she burns time itself.*

In five clicks, Raquel had reached her target, and with a twirl of her wrist, she plucked the empty vessel from the table. Another five clicks and she was back at the bar. Miguel did not know what she was doing behind him, but he heard two more distinct clicks before she was returning to the table with a fresh drink. She was not taking normal steps. Even in that stopped time, she appeared to glide between footfalls.

On her return path, she put her hand back on Miguel's shoulder and pressed down. Her crimson aura flowed over him. The heat of time being forced to remain still blazed all around him. As she released his shoulder, the crimson aura withdrew, and a cool sensation spread over his body as he completed his backward step. Motion continued around the bar, like nothing had happened. The only things that had changed were that Raquel now stood beside him instead of behind the bar and the customer's drink was refilled. Miguel shuddered at how much had happened between instants.

"Amazing," he whispered. "Terrifying, but amazing." His mind was still trying to play out what he had witnessed, but even memory could not play back the speed and motion in its proper time. Thoughts were too slow.

"Usually I don't take that long," she remarked with a slight grin. "But I don't show people my wings often."

He wheezed out a breath, exhausted despite not having moved. When he could breathe without pain, Miguel turned back to the bar. "Wouldn't it be faster not to mix a drink? I mean, it's all the same thing, right? Just that happy juice?"

Raquel snorted. “Happy juice, huh? That’s a new one.” With a shake of her head, she picked up a fresh glass, giving it a playful toss before starting to clean it.

For a full minute, she cleaned and inspected the glass, turning it this way and that. At her satisfaction, Raquel looked at him through the crystal-clear surface. “It’s all about effort. That is part of the mission. The more you put into it, the more people get out of it. The ‘happy juice’ is just a liquid, a base for the proper drink. It is the effort we add into it that makes it what the customers need. Drinking it directly would blow your mind—literally.”

Miguel gave a weak laugh but stopped when Raquel did not do the same. “At some point, I hope someone here starts making sense. I’m no drink-mixer.”

“Mixologist,” she corrected. “Things make more sense as you experience them. A little nudge sometimes helps.” Setting down a series of glasses she had cleaned while they were talking, Raquel nodded at him. “You’re not so bad, Miguel.”

“For a human, you mean?”

Raquel tilted her head, squinting in concentration. “No, just overall not so bad. You’re the type of person I wouldn’t *want* to hit.”

“But you’ve hit me already,” he remarked, his arm recalling the soreness from earlier. *Although it makes sense why she hated hearing me say ‘what the hell’ earlier.*

“Yeah,” she replied with a fond nod at the memory, “but you deserved it. No, you’re probably the first person in a long time I don’t want to punch without cause.”

“Do you punch many people? People you shouldn’t be hitting?”

Raquel shrugged. A new assortment of glassware requiring cleaning had appeared on the counter in front of her. “Yes, I mean, I guess. It is why I’m here. Punching a holy man and all.”

“You punched a holy man? Why?”

“He hugged me, and I don’t *do* touching. I didn’t like it. He was so happy to be in heaven he didn’t stop, so I made him comply in the way I thought was most efficient. Raphael wasn’t happy. So I’m here.” During their conversation, she had cleaned the stack of glasses and had searched for something else to occupy her time. “Anyway, it’s time you go.”

“Go? But I thought we were having a good time. Why would—”

The genuine smile returned to her face, and she gave a slight nod of approval. "We all have our jobs tonight. If you stick around, I might end up having to hit you again."

Miguel laughed, again noticing that Raquel did not join in, and started backing away. "Well, I'm glad we could get to a no-hitting point. I think I'll go check out those back rooms, and I'll find someone else you won't want to hit."

"Miracles happen," she replied, nodding as he left.

After one step, he stopped. "You know, Raquel, I think you should talk to the Marias. They are your coworkers, part of your team or squad. Communication was always a big part of my team back home. It might help make them more efficient… more like you."

The angel gave him a nod, considering his words but not treating them with any significance. "Yeah," she offered back. "Like I need advice from a dead guy."

"Okay, I should go. I've got a lot to do and need all the time I can get," Miguel said with a wave as an open palm slammed onto his back and sent him skidding forward into the crowds.

Raquel's voice chimed into his ear, as clear as if she had been standing beside him. A chill ran down his spine as he realized she literally could stand at his side and he would never have known. "A nudge from an angel to send you on your way."

Chapter 7: The Dance Floor

Driven forward by Raquel's "gentle nudge," Miguel skidded to a halt just short of the stage. *If that's Raquel's method of a gentle send-off, I'm glad she's not out to get me.* Inspecting himself, he was glad to confirm all his parts were present and accounted for, including his clothes. On the room's far side, Raquel had returned to cleaning her glassware. *Thankfully, there weren't any tables in the way. Hitting a table at that speed...* He shuddered at the idea, forcing his brain to dismiss it. After several failed attempts, the image of him cut in half by a table finally subsided.

Walking farther into the room, he noticed the unique events going on at every table. They were like little islands, nestled together but independent. If every life was a small island, then the Día De Muertos theme was like water flowing around it, supplying anything needed for the experience but not controlling it. There was a tug from every table he passed, like the current was trying to pull him to land, yet Miguel resisted.

As he moved between tables, attempting to focus on not bumping into anyone or anything, a tingling sensation ran down his spine. It reminded him of the silver-blue things that watched him earlier. Craning his neck in a wide circle, he tried to locate any of the wispy shapes, but none presented themselves. *They're out there. But where?*

Miguel's steps slowed, and tension gripped his chest. The air's temperature dropped, and his breath came out in steamy plumes. The Morose called out to him, trying to take hold of him and drag him to the ground. *It would all be so simple. Just sit back. Stop struggling.*

"Miguel," a voice called out, snapping him back to attention. "Miguel, my friend, over here!" He spun around to follow the voice, seeing Juan Pedro motion for him from over at the stage. With a dizzy nod, he started making his way through the crowd, taking great pains to avoid colliding with anyone.

I really do not want to get drawn into another celebration, especially not here. People danced, swayed, and sang with the band, creating an impressive obstacle of arms, legs, and bodies. Ducking under one dancing person, Miguel caught another's arm with his face. The arm passed right through his head, but he still flinched. *Just because they don't need me in their party doesn't mean I want arms going through my head.* He glanced back at the stage, Juan Pedro motioning for him to hurry. He sighed, taking a step forward. *Still, I've only got one night.* With that, he walked through a young man, not bothering to avoid him. Every instinct screamed to dodge, to move out of the way, but he strode forward without hesitation. He held his breath as he walked, unsure if it helped, but it gave him something to focus on. Reaching the stage, he let out a shaky breath. The tingling sensation of moving through so many people sent shudders through him.

"Why don't you come up and play with us?" Juan Pedro smiled and gestured to a waiting guitar at the back of the stage. "Tonight is the night for fun and excitement. Come join Juan Pedro on the stage."

“No, no!” Miguel replied. “I don’t play. I mean, I’ve strummed a guitar once or twice, but that was years ago, and that was my wedding, where people were just being polite.”

“Playing is only one part physical, amigo. It’s passion that drives the hand.”

Miguel shook his head. “Maybe later. I’m on a mission right now.”

Juan Pedro nodded, giving Miguel a solemn look. “I’ll hold you to that, amigo. Juan Pedro does not forget a promise.”

For a moment, Miguel stood and watched the man take his place on the stage. Juan Pedro was born to be an entertainer, eager for the spotlight and possessing a child-like level of energy. Even watching him was exhausting. He was a living personality, a spirit of celebration, drawing ecstatic screams from the audience. They transitioned through genres of music without missing a beat. One minute they played a growling rock song. The next, smooth country and then classic jazz. Through it all, none of them showed any sign of slowing or ever stopping.

Miguel stepped from the stage and onto the dance floor, determined to escape to the rec rooms with haste.

"I have seen many dances over many years, but never any like that before. What do you call it?" Muertos's voice called out.

He turned, expecting to find the hostess just over his shoulder, but she was not there. Instead, Madame Muertos had approached him from the front, surprising him by not surprising him.

"I wasn't really dancing, just trying to get out of the way of the music."

She threw her head back into a laugh, a rich, sultry sound from deep within her. There was nothing fake or sinister in the laugh, only a deep mirth. "Then I would be extremely interested to hear the music you were listening to. Here." She held out one gloved hand. "Let me show you how to dance."

Muertos glided into a starting position, one hand raised above her head and the other beckoning Miguel forward. "I assume you know the tango, yes?"

"Oh no, I…" he protested, backing down, but her hand grasped his, and she pulled him in close.

“Have I not been an excellent hostess, Miguel? Would you really deny a lady a dance?” She loomed over him, a larger-than-life presence. That familiar but fleeting memory returned but continued to elude him.

“I don’t want to keep you from your duties. You have important things to do, I’m sure.”

“Nonsense. If you do not know, then let me teach you. I would not be much of a hostess if I did not help you enjoy your stay, yes?” At this distance, he could make out all the full, vibrant colors of her makeup, the twisting swirls of paint, and how her steel eyes glittered with emerald flame. The fires no longer consumed all of her eyes, having diminished to only cover half. Her perfume was as sweet as summer flowers. The scent drew him in, begging him to get closer, to stay with her always.

Then Juan Pedro spoke. “Ah, it seems we have a special request from the lady of the house.” The music changed, becoming faster, filled with a staccato of pops.

Miguel would have complained aloud and cursed Juan Pedro for this betrayal, but there was no time. Muertos took the lead, and Miguel followed.

Using everything he had, he moved in time with Muertos. He tried to match the music, but it was too fast, too energetic. His feet felt two sizes bigger as he stumbled his way around the dance floor. For once, he was grateful that he could pass through others since otherwise he would have been a wrecking ball that sent people flying. Instead, he looked like a man caught in a whirlwind.

Muertos moved with precision, practice, and perfection, each pose locking in place. Even when she dodged his trudging feet, she moved with style, intent, and purpose. The music and Muertos had a strange symbiosis. The more the intensity of the music built up, the more Muertos seemed to command the attention of those around them, which made the music even more noticeable. As if they had rehearsed it, people formed a wide circle around them. The crowds turned and clapped, shouting out whooping cheers. Miguel's face turned from a bright pink to a scarlet red as more people were being drawn into *his* celebration. Not only could they see him, but they were celebrating him. *Is this something I'm doing, or is it because of Muertos?*

The speed of the music grew faster and faster, with Muertos always one step ahead. She moved with a wild passion, perfect precision, and raw energy. Despite her wild motions, not a single hair came out of place. Her hat's pompoms swayed with her motions, like tiny dancers circling her head. He locked eyes on them, tracking their movements. To his surprise, it helped, like these cotton balls were putting the dance instructions into his mind. *Is this me or a function of this place? Can I dance now, or is it making me?*

"You're doing it!" Muertos roared with immense approval, and despite his nervousness, he smiled. Then he laughed. His eyes closed for a moment, and he recalled an image of the last time he danced.

It had been at his wedding, when he and Vanessa shared their first dance as a married couple. She was the spinning ballerina, and he was the stumbling fool. *The more things change.* He smiled. So many loved ones had been there for that moment, a proper celebration of life, and Miguel's smile deepened. *I'm the one out here dancing. If this house is helping me, so be it, but this dance is my choice.*

All around them, couples joined in, dancing and whooping as they tangoed. Yet no one moved with the precision and timing of the hostess. With the striking of the last notes, she grabbed Miguel's hand, throwing their arms upward before plunging him into a bow. The change in direction nearly threw him face-first into the floor.

The crowd went wild with applause and shouts. Miguel nodded at the people who walked by, patting his shoulder and complimenting Muertos on her skill. She brushed off their praise with a faint, "Oh, I dance a little."

As the next song started up, he regarded the hostess. "Why make an extra effort to help me? I mean, lots of people do not dance. I can't be the only one."

"No, but you were the one who seemed to call out for my help." She arched an eyebrow at him. "Would you care to dance again? You were stepping on the floor much more than my feet by the end of our dance."

He sighed in exhaustion. "No, no, no. I need something a little more relaxed. I'll go sit at the bar for—"

She waved a hand, cutting him off. “Plenty of time for bars and drinks later. Why not check out the gaming area if you want something calmer? While it’s not my cup of tea, the Marias tell me the rec room is ‘totally cool.’”

“I’d have to find them first, and I’m afraid I’ve gotten myself all turned around with dancing and everything.”

“Well then.” Muertos grinned, pointing over his head. “I suppose it’s a good thing we’re already here.”

Chapter 8: Green Means "Go"

Miguel entered the recreation rooms and shielded his eyes against the blinding light. While the ballroom area was neat and decorated for a celebration, compared to this area, the bar looked shady and dingy. It was a large square room, reminding him of a community center. Three hallways branched off from the room, each illuminated by either green, blue, or purple light. In the center of the room was a kiosk with a small sign reading *Help Station.*

Approaching the kiosk, he leaned forward to ring the small bell on the counter. In a pastel green shimmer, Lima Maria appeared before him, close enough that their noses almost touched. Leaning away, Miguel took a few reflexive steps backward. This gave him a moment to take in her full appearance. She wore the same uniform as the other Marias: white top, colored skirt, and headband to hold back her long dark hair. However, Lima's attire was frantic, giving her the look of someone who had gotten dressed in a hurry, perhaps even in the dark. Her top's buttons went into the wrong holes, leaving a lone button dangling. The lime green headband shifted on her head, losing the battle to keep her hair from falling into her face. Her attention darted from the gathering back behind her. She bit her lip and swallowed hard. The most captivating and interesting thing was her eyes. They flashed with brilliant light, the color matching her lime green skirt. It was not a steady, static color akin to normal eyes; instead, they raced in a circular motion like a trapped comet seeking an escape route.

"H-h-hello, sir," she sputtered. "Did you need help?" Her foot tapped with nervous energy, adding to the growing sense of urgency in her posture. The pastel green light spinning in her eyes flickered, swerving from the course set by her irises but snapping back into line. She opened her mouth and prepared to say something else, and Miguel knew he needed to speak now or he would never get a word in.

"Oh, um, yes, hello," Miguel replied. "So what is this place? What can I do here?"

"This is the recreational zone, the 'rec rooms.'" She paused for a microsecond to make air quotes around the room's name. "Here you can find any hobby needed for a Death Night Festival. What's a Death Night Festival? Well—"

"Muertos already explained that. I just want to know—"

She nodded and gave a sound of agreement before continuing. “Well then, do you want to watch your favorite movie? We have 1200 theaters, 820 private screening rooms, a concession stand with snacks from anywhere you can and can’t imagine. No alcohol, though. Liquor licenses are such a pain. Red tape and all that. Although you would think Raquel should be able to get it.” She let out another quick laugh. It was unsettling, as her tone rose and fell in a frantic, jarring way. “We also have—”

“Okay, but why? Why break it up into separate rooms?”

“Because it’s everyone’s party. No matter what they want. We are ready for any kind of party, anywhere, anytime. Kind of like a resort more than a bar. Oh! I think Juan Pedro said that once.” The energy in her eyes skipped, rising from and then falling back onto the surface of her eyes. Her head twitched for a moment before she gave it a shake and looked back at him. “I guess you knew that, since you were there. What wouldn’t you know? Hm, oh! Did you know we even have rooms for reading if you want to sit in silence with friends and read a book? I suppose not, since you’re asking me.” Another pause for a laugh, this one the inverse of her previous. “A-a-although most who do that prefer the veranda and patios. You can get to those down the halls over there." Lima Maria pointed at a series of hallways on her left. "There are signs. Look for Violeta's lights—those are the purple ones—to get outside. Green is my color." She grabbed her skirt, giving him an abrupt curtsy. "They go to all the game rooms. Games of pool, card games, gyms, and a lot more. I could list them all. Would you like me to do that?"

"No," he gasped. While she had been the one talking, Miguel was the one who felt out of breath. "I'll just take a peek around, thanks." Turning, he headed toward the nearest hallway.

Lima Maria screamed, horror and mad panic in her voice. "Not that way!"

Miguel froze. "Why not?" he whispered. "What's wrong?"

"That's the way to the blue rooms," Lima Maria added. The terror had left her voice, replaced by her normal jittery cadence. "Avoid the blue rooms."

"Why?" He stretched the word out to hide the growing panic in his voice.

"Well, t-that hall leads to Azul Maria's stations, because they are blue. Blue is her color, like how the green areas are mine. She watches over everyone there, including the b-b-b—" The last word stuck in her throat, mind and mouth missing a connection along the way. Lima drew in a deep, ragged breath. When she spoke, it was calm and deliberate, with an eerie sense of stillness. "You probably wouldn't like it. Most of us try to stay out of her way back there. It's…" She stopped, a twitch in her eye as she processed the right word. "Unsettling and not what you want to see."

"Okay," Miguel replied, "I won't go to the blue rooms." Lima beamed a nervous smile. With the conversation complete, her gaze drifted around the room, following another of those sounds or sights no one else could hear. Then, since he had not left in that split second, she turned her glowing green eyes on him.

There was something in them, in her manic demeanor, that confused him. On the one hand, he wanted to escape her random chaotic presence, but on the other, her frantic behavior was a wonder to behold. *I should leave. I've got to find a purpose or celebrate my festival. I can't stop to talk to the help. Raquel might even put me in a headlock if I do.* He examined the disheveled woman. The image of the woman running from his office returned to his mind. *Saying something has only caused me trouble.*

He turned but stopped as a tug pulled on his heart. *Still…* Miguel cleared his throat. "Miss Lima Maria, are you okay? Did I say something wrong?"

"N-n-no," she replied, her voice faltering. "That's so very nice of you to ask. I'm just doing my job. No problems here. I mean, V-V-Violeta says I drink too much coffee, but it smells *so* good. How could I help it? Plus, it helps me stay focused. I think it helps me stay focused. Don't you think so? I think so. I—"

"Coffee?"

She nodded hard enough that Miguel expected her head to pop off. "Oh, didn't I tell you? I also run the concession and coffee shop back here." Lima pointed to a full assortment of snacks and a barista station. Miguel raised an eyebrow but was no longer surprised by something new appearing. "Would you like something?" Lima Maria gave him a smile, and the energy flowing in her eyes settled. No longer bouncing around her irises, it slowed and flowed in a steady path.

Her smile was infectious, and Miguel mirrored her grin. “Sure, you only live once, right?”

“What can I get you? I can make anything you like, and I can make anything you don’t like, but I don’t know why you’d ask for that.”

“Surprise me.” Miguel laughed to himself. If there was one thing the night was good at, it was surprising him. *What’s one more, right?*

Lima laughed with a little less mania before pulling on an apron with patchwork pockets and going to work behind the counter. She was fast, her motions a blur and a whirl of activities, but there was none of Raquel's precision or grace. She moved fast enough that she appeared to be in multiple places at once, each Lima at a different location. One pressed the coffee, another frothed foam, and another grabbed various spices and flavorings. At one point, it appeared as though two of them might have been arguing about something, but then, with a pop, they flowed into a single Lima Maria and all the coffee components fell together. With a proud smile, she held out the cup of coffee. It was a bizarre concoction topped high with whipped cream, caramel, and chocolate sprinkles, everything colored lime green.

"Thank you, I—" As he reached out to take the cup, she let it go. To Miguel's surprise, it did not fall, instead floating in the air as Lima fumbled through every apron pocket until she produced a marker. With a flourish, she scribbled on the side, popped the cap back on the marker, and dropped it back into a different pocket. Then, as if the cup were resting on a shelf, she plucked it from the air and handed it to Miguel.

"C-c-careful not to drop it."

"Drop it? But it was just floating."

"Oh, that's because it's a little pick-me-up." She giggled, laughing at her own pun. Her laugh reminded Miguel of something he'd heard in a haunted house. She seemed to have a variety of mannerisms and laughs, all of which she had used in every conversation. "That's not the name, though. No, I call this drink the Casual Walk. I have one before I do my room checks."

"How often is that?" he asked, taking a quick sniff of the drink. He could make out caramel, vanilla, and some fusion of cinnamon and chocolate, but then there was some other ingredient he could not place.

She beamed. "I'm always checking the rooms."

"Ah," Miguel replied, raising the cup in a gesture of thanks. "Well, it smells… wonderful. I'm sure it's delicious." For once, she did not say a word, but the way her eyes widened in anticipation spoke volumes. *Oh no, she wants me to drink this now. I was hoping to get it and go.* Bracing himself, Miguel decided he would take a small sip, but only enough to be polite. While he often drank coffee in the morning, it had never been a favorite of his.

One sip and Miguel understood how plants got their energy from the sun. The liquid Lima Maria called coffee was pure energy. No sooner had it entered his mouth than energy surged through him with the force of lightning striking his tongue. Jittery power coursed into his body, and Miguel expected to blow up like an old light bulb. Lima stepped in front of him, saying something that Miguel could not hear over the sound of his heart beating like a jackhammer in his ears. He watched her lips moving, seeing them enunciate each syllable. *This must be how hummingbirds live.*

He let out what he thought was a slow breath, but to his ears, it sounded like a hurricane blowing out a candle. *Focus, Miguel.* He closed his eyes, but they popped back open. His body moved too fast for even momentary rest. He tried again, forcing his eyes shut. *Focus*, he repeated. *You can do this. It's just a little… caffeine? Sugar? Nuclear waste?* Images of every energetic item he could imagine danced across his mind's eye. He took another breath, this time letting it out in an even and steady cadence. As his eyes flickered open, Miguel coughed. His throat was raw. Lima watched him, her head ratcheting to the side as she waited for his answer.

"I'm sorry," he said, his voice a hoarse whimper. "What was that?"

"I asked if you wanted me to add more sugar. It's kind of bland, I know." Lima reached out to take the drink.

"No." He coughed. The beverage had the same pleasing effect as the bar's food and drink, only ramped up with caffeine and raw power. *What is this?* Miguel drew the coffee back from her, afraid of what the energetic woman would deem the correct amount of sugar. "No, it's fine."

Lima seemed confused. "No *more* sugar? Well, suit yourself." She placed the sugar behind the counter and then returned to her uncomfortably close spot before him. He wondered how worn the soles of her shoes must be from the sudden stops. "Anything else I can do for you, Mr. Miguel?"

"No, I think… I should go have a look around. Uh, thank you for the coffee. I'll see you around again, okay, Lima?"

She perked up, her random energy compelling her to stand straight. "That would be great. I'd enjoy that."

Moving apart, they exchanged nods. Miguel was not sure when he should stop nodding. Once he had stepped into a hallway, seeing the green lights along the floor, he turned to get his bearings. By the time he peered back at the kiosk, Lima Maria had disappeared, returning to her rounds. Miguel regarded his drink. While he was not sure he would drink any more of it, the cup acted like a lightning rod to ground him. Even through the cardboard sleeve, it pulsed with radiance and heat, but it was a steady presence as he navigated the corridor lit with emerald lights.

As Lima had said, there were rooms for any activity he could imagine. Movie theaters, arcades, even courts where people played team sports. He paused as he passed one gymnasium, then returned to look back through the glass opening on the door. *Is that a baseball diamond? Inside?* Holding up a hand in defeat, he moved on.

What am I looking for? What kind of purpose or celebration would I find in a game room? Miguel thought about his hobbies, his interests. Neither he nor Vanessa played any games besides the occasional hand of cards with friends, but with none of them present, a card game would not be the same. *What do I do for fun, then?* While he absently took a sip of his drink, energy coursed through his limbs, and he put that power into moving forward as fast as he could. Within a few seconds, he was covering large portions of ground with each step. He came to a corner and twisted to avoid slamming into a wall. In two more steps, he was at another turn. Unable to get his feet under him, this time he hit the wall. Miguel did not stop upon impact. Instead, the wall shifted into a set of doors and he rolled into a conference room filled with tables and crowds of people. Unlike Miguel, the Casual Walk did not appear shaken or to have spilled. If drinks could laugh, he imagined the coffee would be cackling.

As he struggled to his feet, heart slowing since he had burned off some energy, Miguel stared at the green liquid. Then, pleased but a little surprised it *did not* laugh, he turned to take in the room. As he expected, no one noticed his sudden and dramatic entrance. *I'm glad that's not part of anyone's celebration.*

The room turned out to be a great convention hall, well-lit and clean. Round tables were organized into sections with enough room for plenty of people to sit around them. But it was the ceiling that caught Miguel's attention. Above them all were skylights showing a night sky unlike anything he had seen before. The sky was packed with planets of every color whose moons orbited fast enough that he could see them move, and a myriad of stars blinked in the darkness between everything.

It makes sense that the world outside would also change. Why would it be any different? Shaking his head, he returned his attention to the room. People played a variety of games, some with dice, others with cards or plastic pieces. Something in this room called to him. Not the games themselves, but he almost thought he could hear someone calling out to him. *I guess a look around couldn't hurt.* He checked his knees, half expecting to see them covered in scuffs and bruises from his fall.

Drifting between the tables, he tried watching the various games. However, none of them made any sense. Everything was gibberish to his ears, and he kept moving. There was still a prickling sensation on the back of his neck, the feeling he would get when someone was watching over his shoulder. Everyone seemed to enjoy themselves. Occasionally, someone new would step up to a table, and the others would cheer, commenting about the fact that they had been waiting, although from what Miguel saw, that was never the case. Laughter rang out at some shared jokes; people drank soda instead of beers, ales, and mixed drinks like in the greater ballroom. Instead of platters of food and entire meals, there were snacks and chips, which he recognized from Lima's concession.

Miguel searched the room, wondering if Lima was here right now. Finding an open seat, he sat next to an older man sorting through a stack of cards. There was something familiar about him, but Miguel could not place the face. *Typical*, he thought, stopping himself from taking another sip of his coffee.

"Care for a game?" The older man smiled, his face brightening as he noticed Miguel.

“Oh, no.” Miguel waved him off. “No, this game looks too complicated for me.”

The man gave a weak chuckle. “I hear that a lot. My son said the same thing when I tried to teach him. It’s not too hard. Plus”—he gestured around—“we are all here to play. Why not join in on the fun?”

“I suppose I could play a game. I mean, how long could it take?”

“Famous last words.” The man chuckled again and extended his hand. “Steven.”

“Miguel,” he answered, taking the offered hand. Again, Miguel felt a familiarity for the man. Yet try as he might, he could not place Steven. *Do I even know a Steven?*

Steven pulled a second stack of cards from one of the many pockets on his worn backpack and explained the function of various features on them. Miguel nodded, forcing himself to focus on listening. He set down his Casual Walk and slid it away. *Getting a paper cut at the speed a Casual Walk puts me in could remove a hand.*

The game was not something Miguel would have ever picked up on his own. The rules often seemed overcomplicated and to contradict themselves, but Steven spoke with such passion that Miguel enjoyed the simple act of listening to him.

At one point, a piece of paper appeared beside Steven, who jotted down numbers and information. Miguel chuckled to himself. *Why didn't I think of that? Writing things down might help me out.* Beside him, a pad of paper and pen appeared. *Just like what I use at the office.*

"I forgot I put *that* card in the deck," Steven remarked, and Miguel looked away from his fresh conjuring. "My son used to play it all the time. I can't tell you how many times I lost to that thing."

"Is your son here now?" Miguel asked, scanning for any newcomers. Muertos might have called this a festival for the dead, but he was thinking it was really a home for haunted house jump-scare enthusiasts.

Steven moved cards around in his hand, not meeting Miguel's eyes. "No. No, he's not. I was on my way to see him and his family. I was driving over after a doctor's visit. You know how those go, always bad news. Traffic was a little congested…" The man paused, confused, as he played a card from his hand.

Miguel responded to his play with his own, pleased that he had learned enough to do something.

"Nice move," Steven said with a distracted tone. "You will think this is weird, but do I know you?"

"You know, I had a similar feeling about you."

"Yeah. Yeah." Steven chewed on the words. "You live around here?"

Miguel tugged on his ear, unsure of how to answer. *Live around here? That would be a hard thing to say.* He studied the older man again, taking in his features. The concern and confusion on Steven's face was so familiar, so recent, so… Miguel sighed; he knew where he recognized Steven. *I stepped out into the road and was hit by a car.* He could see Steven behind the wheel, that same look on his face. Anger welled in Miguel's chest. *He hit me with his car. He killed me.*

His emotions flaring, Miguel was unsure what to do or even what he wanted to do. He was dead, and his murderer now sat across from him, playing card games and making jokes. Acting like he had done nothing wrong at all.

Above, the celestial sky flashed, multicolored lightning shooting between the planets. For the first time, everyone in the room turned their attention upward to acknowledge the outside world. *Good*, he fumed. *Good. It's about time people started seeing things besides themselves. I* died *because of this man. I'll never see my wife and family again.* Outside, the wind howled, and the room shook. Pieces on various tables clattered to the ground, and people fell from their seats.

Steven was not looking at Miguel, instead mirroring everyone else to regard the raging storm above. Miguel rose to his feet, sliding his chair back with a screech. Glowering down at Steven, he struggled to find the right damning words to hurl at his killer. The older man turned, perhaps sensing the rage coming from Miguel or just startled by the sudden movement. As Steven turned, he shoved his backpack, causing a small white bottle to roll free. Miguel's eyes fixed on it.

Steven's words echoed in his head. *Doctor's visits. You know how those go, always bad news.*

Muertos's words returned to him. *We do not tell people they are dead. It is up to them to come to terms with their fate and move on. That is not our place or purpose. We are servants of the recently deceased. We guide and aid, not order and instruct.*

Would that be the ultimate revenge? Telling him he was dead? That he killed me? Yeah, it would mess him up. His mind drifted back to Raquel, to how she had reacted when she thought he was calling her "not fun." *Would it have the same effect on him? Would it shatter his fun and give him the Morose?*

He turned back to the bottle, seeing the prescription label. One word stood out as it rolled to a halt.

Heart.

Miguel let out a breath halfway between a groan and a shout. *A heart attack. He died of a heart attack while going to see family.*

"You okay, Miguel?" Steven asked, reaching out a hand to support the shaking man.

“Yeah,” he replied in a near-inaudible whisper. “Yeah, I’ll be fine. Just a little shaken up.” Miguel shook his head, then pointed to the skylight. He still wanted to scream, to shout at Steven, but his emotions were all jumbled up inside of him.

From what Miguel could understand, he would lose on his next turn. With nothing left to do, he passed the active turn to the older man. When Steven moved to finish the game, Miguel would reveal what he knew. *Lose the battle but win the war.*

Steven took a moment to study the game, the cards in his hand, and then Miguel. The more experienced player smiled, selected a card from his hand, and played it for his turn. Reading it over, Miguel frowned. “Steven, that doesn’t seem like a good idea. This card, it would not help you. Wouldn’t that let me win? Why give up your advantage?”

“You must not be a parent, right? Sometimes we do things to show support, even if it loses us the game. Winning isn’t everything, right? Besides, if I beat you now, would you want to keep playing?”

Miguel flexed his hand, remembering the sensation of a plastic bag tight against his fingers. *A parent.* The word echoed in his mind. Then he looked back to Steven. "Helping others…" His heart winced. "Thank you," he replied in a whisper. "I almost made a mistake, but… well… thank you."

Steven furrowed his brow, confused by Miguel's confession, then shook his head before glancing at his watch with a groan. "Would you look at the time? Here I am, talking your ear off and playing games when I *need* to be hitting the road. Traffic is probably better now."

"Yeah," Miguel grunted, "I'm sure it'll be a smooth ride home for you. No bumps in the road."

Steven reached out a hand, and Miguel returned the gesture.

"Miguel. Been a pleasure. Have a splendid night. I hope we can play again sometime." With a last nod, Steven walked to the game room doors and faded away.

Miguel watched the spot where Steven had vanished, his emotions still roiling. *I wanted to scream at him. Why didn't I? I could have gotten my revenge for—*

For what? he asked himself. *For an accident? Revenge?*

Picking up the pen, he started scribbling random words and phrases on his pad of paper. The act of writing felt good, even if it was just putting random thoughts and words to paper. He wrote until his hand cramped, and he was forced to set the pen down to examine his work. Mostly it was a series of jumbled phrases, but three words stood out. *When to speak?*

With a groan, he crumpled the page and tossed it aside, the paper ball rolling and disappearing a short distance away. With a final groan, he collected his coffee and rose, leaving the game room. Unlike Steven, however, he did not move on. His mind was still a storm of emotions, but walking the winding hallways helped burn off some of his angry energy.

"E-everything okay, Mr. Miguel?" Lima blurted as she appeared almost on top of him again. He jerked back, unsure if he would collide with her since she, too, could interact with things.

"Everything is *fine*, Lima," he growled, trying to step past her and resume his angry walking. For every move he made, she countered, always staying right before him. He stepped back, putting out a hand that seemed to convince her not to get back into his immediate personal space. "I'm trying to figure out what to do next.

card games are fun and all, but not really my thing."

"Oh, yes. I saw you learning to play. Most people don't learn new games when they're here. They just focus on what they knew before. Isn't that weird you learned something? Kind of a fun fact. Did you know that guy? I guess if you knew him, he could teach you something, but I have never seen that before. Kind of weird you met someone you didn't know again, but at least you didn't fall into a cake this time. Weird storm in there, too." She dissected everything Miguel had said and done in the game room in a happy, matter-of-fact tone. Her eyes glowing with a genuine sense of curiosity, Lima appeared eager to hear his answers, even if she was not leaving enough time for a response.

"Lima, *please*," he snapped as his residual agitation seeped into his voice. She stopped and recoiled from him. Miguel's anger faded, replaced with guilt as he remembered his own written words: *when to speak*. "I'm sorry, Lima. I shouldn't have snapped at you."

"No, I-I-I'm sorry." She sniffed, her little frame quivering. "I know I c-can come on strong. Violeta says I'm just a j-ji-jitterbug, but I don't want to screw up and make someone a Lost One. I don't mean to upset you." Tears welled in those vibrant green eyes, and she swallowed down a lump.

When to speak. He rubbed his temples. *Should I be talking or not?* he asked himself. Seeing the tears rolling down her cheeks, Miguel raised his hands in the best soothing gesture he could muster. "Lima, Lima, it's okay. You're doing great. I wasn't mad at you."

"B-but I screwed up. I—"

Placing one hand on her shoulder, he focused on his speaking. *Slow down. Think.* She trembled, twitching where his hand touched. "You didn't screw up. I just met someone I didn't want to see."

"Was it me?" she blurted, a tear racing in a jagged pattern down her cheek. "I'm supposed to make people happy, to bring them joy. But I'm always so… nervous that I react too fast. I wish I could relax like Azul or be confident like Violeta. I'm not good at my purpose, and I—"

Lima stopped. The erratic green light that whirled in her eyes became smoke gray, and the skin under Miguel's hand had become still and cold. Her legs crumpled, and Miguel fumbled to catch her as she fell to the floor. Coffee splashed from his cup, throwing whipped cream all over them.

"Lima!" he shouted, guiding her to rest on the ground. "Lima," he repeated in a whisper, unsure if he should call out for help and stay with her or go out to find someone. He doubted anyone would hear him over the noise in the bar, and he wasn't sure how he would explain the situation. "Please don't go. I didn't mean to yell at you. I wasn't mad at you. You did nothing wrong." A weak attempt at a laugh escaped his lips. "I couldn't even bring myself to yell at him, but I yelled at you. What kind of man does that make me?" Since she offered no answer, he continued. "Not a good one. I don't know when to speak and when to keep my mouth shut."

Lima Maria felt smaller now, like a piece of her was no longer there. He could not be sure if it was the vacant expression in her eyes or the chill of her skin against his arms, but on some level, she was fading away.

“I might not know when to speak, Lima, but I’d like you to say something right now.” Miguel sighed, trying to remove a small blob of green whipped cream from her hair, hoping he could at least help in that small way, but all he did was smear it further into her hair. He chuckled. “I made a mess of your hair and the drink you gave me. I’m sorry, Lima.” Miguel stretched out his legs, shifting her in his arms. “What do you say? Wake up and give me one more chance?”

A spark of green light ran a quick circuit in her eyes.

“Lima!” he sobbed, sitting her up. “Lima, are you there?”

She blinked, first one eye and then the other. After a few seconds, both eyes blinked in unison. “What do you mean? I… Oh, did I stop?”

He moved back, helping her up. “Yes… you stopped. You got cold. I thought… Well, I thought you were dead.”

Lima Maria regarded him with a curious gleam in her eyes. “Dead? I cannot die since I’m not alive. I am part of the house and the party and all that. I must have messed up again.”

"No, no, you didn't," Miguel repeated. "I messed up. I took my anger out on you. I met the man who killed me, and I was mad. You probably thought I was mad at you, but—"

Lima gave a laugh, a bizarre, nervous cackle of random sounds and pitches that bordered on a shriek of panic. "Oh, that makes sense, then. You must have been mad, and I thought you were mad at me. Then I thought I failed my purpose and went inert. Then I got back up, and you told me what happened. Then I started telling you…"

Miguel smiled as she recited the events a few more times. At the very least, Lima was back.

She paused again, taking a breath between sentences. "Why are you talking to me? No other guests do. They never even know I'm here. Why are you seeing me so much?"

"I don't know," he answered. "I guess I needed someone to talk to."

She considered those words, looking at him without understanding. "But I never talk to people. You could talk to Raquel or Muertos, even Juan Pedro. Violeta says we're not supposed to bother guests or intrude on their celebrations."

"Well, it's okay with me. We all need someone to talk to sometimes, and if you want to talk, you talk as much as you want. Besides, Violeta isn't here. For now, you're part of my celebration."

A meek smile crossed her face.

"Here," Miguel said, pulling a napkin from his pocket to wipe the remaining whipped cream from her hair. *I'm getting better at making stuff.* He smiled in satisfaction.

Lima blushed, then looked at the drink in his hand. "Don't you like it? You haven't drank much of it. I could make you something else if you don't like it. It's my favorite, but it's okay if—"

Knowing he would regret it, but knowing he might not convince her otherwise, Miguel took a big drink of the Casual Walk, bypassing the straw and coating his face in thick whipped cream and green sprinkles. Where the cream touched his face, Miguel felt a tingling sensation. *What exactly is in this drink?*

Lima giggled in a calm and pleased voice. “You’ve got a little… over… well…” She made a circle in the air, indicating most of his face. As a nuclear reactor went off in his chest, Lima reached out with her own light green handkerchief. “Can’t have a guest making a mess of himself,” she offered. Her hand was steady, and he wondered if she was calming down or if he was moving so fast that she appeared still.

“Thank you,” he offered. “Now, I need to walk off this energy.” He held out an arm. “Lima, I don’t have all night to learn about this place, so could you be my guide for a while? It would just be a *casual walk*, if you have time.”

She beamed, taking his arm. With a crackle in their steps, they rocketed down the various green hallways, stopping for a moment to look in on the guests. In the blink of an eye, they were in the reading rooms, where people sat back to back, reading their favorite novels. There was a warm comfort to the action, and while there was not much motion, the room buzzed with a static power. There were the movie theaters, where fans whooped as villains fell and heroes rose. In the board game room, pieces clacked and clicked all around. Each room they visited had its own charm, with unique guests enjoying their night together in the best way they knew how.

By the end of the tour, Miguel had drunk half his coffee and had to force himself not to consume any more for fear of going off like a firework. It might have been hours, but it felt like only a few minutes had passed when Lima released his arm. "I'm sorry, and this has been a lot of fun, but I have to go now."

"What?"

"I am at work, Mr. Miguel, remember? This was a fun walk, but now I need to start again."

He nodded that he understood, even if his brain was having trouble putting it all together. Seeing Lima step away was like watching a part of him walk away.

"Okay, Lima. See you later, then?"

"Goodbye, Mr. Miguel, and thank you. This was fun, more fun than I've had in a long time." Then, in a shimmer of pastel-lime-colored light, she vanished.

Miguel staggered for a moment, his head pounding from the aftereffects of half a Casual Walk and traveling at Lima's speed. It had been fun, and while the distraction had been nice, he was not sure what to do next.

The surrounding air no longer crackled with excited green lightning. Instead, it fell over him with a calm stillness. *After all that excitement, having it end would make me feel a little blue.*

Blue. He noticed the color of the lights. He had entered the one place Lima warned him not to go: the blue rooms.

Chapter 9: Feeling Blue

Miguel turned, determined to leave the blue rooms, but all he could see were blue hallways leading in every direction. *Shouldn't they be green?*

He ran back, expecting to see a branching hallway or a twist that led back to the green area, but no matter how much he ran or willed it, the halls and rooms remained tinted in blue light. At one point, he took another sip of his coffee, letting the surge of power increase his speed. But all that did was get him nowhere faster.

As he was not making any progress, Miguel shifted to a comfortable walking speed and considered his options. The halls had a different vibe from Lima's game rooms. There was no activity or sound, only subdued silence like being in a library. *Or at a wake.* The thought had popped into his mind and did little to bring him comfort.

He walked by room after room but did not look inside any of them. Lima had called it "different," and Miguel feared what he might see inside. Madame Muertos's home could become anything, and if the blue rooms had a reputation of scaring even the servants of death, it must be terrifying.

Curiosity got the better of him, and he glanced into one room. Until now, he had seen old friends and families, soldiers in arms, and lovers reuniting around a table, drinking at Raquel's counter, or dancing to their hearts' content.

This room was unfamiliar, and based on what he was seeing, Miguel could piece together why Azul Maria's rooms had the reputation for being different. The room itself was not upsetting. Even what was happening did not seem so bad at first glance. No one inside was miserable. In fact, seeing everyone so happy was what made it so disturbing.

The blue rooms are for children, for babies. Even the young are not immune.

Inside this room, labeled *Toys* with a backward S, children painted with their fingers and colored pictures before putting them on the walls, little artists hanging their masterpieces. Rainbow-colored chairs and tables, sized for children, filled the room as kids played and painted. No one was sad or crying. Instead, they behaved in the same carefree way they always would have, celebrating their lives with juice boxes, toys, and crayons rather than dancing, games, and drinks.

There were some adults in the room. They sat perched on chairs as the children brought toys from the toy boxes and explained every detail about what the toy was and what it could do.

Bittersweet tears filled his eyes as a woman wiped a smudge of chocolate from a child's mouth, her laugh soulful and cheery. The sound struck a chord with Miguel, and his hand winced from that phantom pain that had been plaguing him all night. Two mysteries remained in his mind: how he knew Muertos and the plastic bag he had been carrying before he died. He knew how he had died, and who had caused his death, but those other details still eluded him.

Not wanting to eavesdrop on this auspicious moment, he continued looking for a way out of the blue rooms. He had seen enough here to last him for a long time.

"Oh, hello." Azul yawned, her words elongated and strained as if they were stretching with her yawn. She walked with a slow and steady pace as she came up beside him. She held an infant wrapped in a blue blanket. "I didn't think you'd want to come back here. Few people wander into the blue rooms. Lima says it's because they are too *different* from the rest of the party. Do you like children, Mr. Miguel?"

There was a calm peace to her stance. The simple act of not moving seemed to be all she needed to be happy. She rotated her neck, smiling at the small cracks and pops that came from her stiff joints. She wore the same uniform as her sisters, but with a blue theme. Whereas Lima Maria's outfit appeared to have been thrown on haphazardly, Azul Maria's clothing draped over her lazily, giving her the look of someone who could not muster the energy to finish getting ready.

Clearing his throat, he thought about the nicest way to say, *No, I want to get out of here. Now. This place creeps me out.* However, nothing came to mind, and he looked for any opening to escape.

Azul did not react to his silence, seeming to enjoy standing still and being quiet. She gave the infant in her arms a gentle bounce and whispered something soothing. Miguel shifted his foot back, preparing to walk away when she turned her head. "Wait a minute. Is that a Casual Walk you have there? Lima makes the *best* coffee." Her gaze was hungry, and he passed her the drink. "You're okay if I have some? I'm not supposed to take things from guests."

He nodded. "Not my cup of tea."

“Oh, I know. Mr. Miguel, it’s coffee, not tea.” There was an obliviousness to her words, but Miguel was more worried that anyone would drink such a volatile concoction on purpose.

“I should warn you,” he started, but in one swift motion, she drained the entire cup. A small green whipped-cream beard formed around her mouth, and she laughed while licking it from her lips.

“Well, isn’t that refreshing?” she said, handing him the empty cup. “Thank you.” Her voice had a more even tone now, and she was speaking at a normal conversational speed. “I’m more awake now, but I see what you were trying to warn me about. Lima just does not know how to add enough sugar. Well, I’ll make sure she puts more in your next cup. It’s lacking that *pop*. Oh, I’m sorry. I shouldn’t have taken the whole thing. I could have her bring you another one. Perhaps something with a little more kick.”

“No,” he interjected, and Azul Maria held up a finger to her mouth, shushing him while nodding at the sleeping infant in her arms. “Um… Azul, why are you carrying a baby?”

"Oh, it's not mine," she answered as if that explained everything. Her eyes twinkled in the blue light, and she rocked the tiny figure. "I'm just getting him ready." Without another word, she turned and walked back down the hall.

Miguel looked behind him. He could turn and run, but where would that get him? The blue hallway seemed to stretch on without end. Here, even time itself did not seem to be in a hurry to move. Ahead, Azul approached a corner.

Is that the end of the hall? He took off after her, eager to escape this place. "Azul! Wait up, please!"

She cast him an exasperated look while making a shushing motion. "Mr. Miguel," she whispered with an angry hiss. "Please, be quiet. If not for me, for the little ones…"

As he closed the last few feet, Miguel heard his steps thunder in the hallway. "Sorry," he whispered back. "I didn't mean it. I'm still acting like I'm at a party."

"Oh, you are. It's merely at a smaller scale." She tickled the infant once again. "Party over here," she cooed in a loud whisper.

Before he could speak, a woman approached them and took the infant from Azul. The woman in blue exchanged a few kind words with the newcomer and waved a quiet goodbye.

"Who was—"

"An ancestor." She yawned with a little click in her jaw. "She came to take that little one home."

"How could you tell?"

The lady in blue rolled her head but made no reply. Instead, she walked to a nearby door and prepared to step inside. "The gate lets me know when the paperwork is completed. I had just finished getting that little one ready when I noticed you in the hall." She investigated the room, then turned back to Miguel. "Would you like to come in? You are welcome to come in, but I must ask that you be quiet."

Miguel hesitated and looked back down the corridors. As far as he could see, the blue lights continued endlessly, and so he followed her into the room. *Maybe this room will connect to another hallway or she can tell me how to get out of here. Besides, how bad can it be? It's just kids, right?* Stepping inside, he saw a room filled with rows of sleeping infants, each resting in their own little crib, an information chart on the side. Some had names written on them. Others did not. "Where are we?"

"This is where I watch the niños and niñas." Her head bowed. "I wait here with them until the gate clears people to come and collect them." She stopped by one fidgeting infant and tickled his stomach with three fingers. The little one laughed, and she smiled back. "It's not as flashy as the others, but it's important someone is there for them." Reaching down, she lifted an infant from his bed. "Want to hold one?"

"No, I'm not good with children. I—" Cutting his protests short, Azul placed the infant in Miguel's arms. His body locked in place as the weight of the child rested in his arms. "Miss Azul Maria, please," he hissed in quiet desperation. "I don't know how to hold—"

“You’re doing just fine,” she encouraged him, making slight adjustments to his arms and hands. “He will not break. Don’t worry so much.” Her laugh was a haunting, slow melody. “I have seen no one so bad with children since Violeta tried this, although the Madame wasn’t much better…”

Somehow, over the course of a few seconds, one of the infant’s legs found its way out of the blanket. He grumbled his discomfort. Around them, the other babies mimicked the grumpiness, and the agitation spread. If something did not happen soon, the entire room would be full of crying babies.

“Uh…” Miguel got out. Half balancing, half holding the baby with one arm, he tried to get the leg back into the blanket, but it was a losing battle. The angle was not right, and he could not see a solution to the problem.

Azul reached out, tickling the underside of the infant’s leg. The baby giggled, and the sound resonated with the others. “There, there, it will be okay.” She reached both arms toward Miguel to take the little one from him.

As she removed the infant from his hands, Miguel clutched his right hand as a slicing pain crossed it. The same phantom pain he had been struggling to identify all night, but now it was several times more intense. With the pain came clarity, and he remembered what the sensation was telling him.

He remembered being at work, how Vanessa had called him. She wanted him to pick up streamers for the party. They had waited until the day of the event to buy them, to ensure they would not ruin the surprise. It was a simple request. "When you're out at lunch, pick up some streamers for the party."

Miguel remembered how he had smiled. How he had told the clerk all about their plans. Then he stepped outside, and then… *Then I was here.*

Then I met Muertos.

The memory pulled back, and the pain subsided. It still hurt, but having a name for the memory made it more tolerable. The strength faded from his legs, and he toppled over. Miguel reached out for something to hold himself up. Azul was beside him, talking about "being careful" and "cribs," but his brain was not registering the information.

The memory of his death came again. Miguel exhaled but then found he could no longer draw in a breath. The air in the room was stagnant, as if it could not move into his lungs. His vision grew dark, and he heaved, trying to force in a breath, but it would not come. With a last effort, he fell to the floor, and everything faded to black.

***

Miguel's eyes fluttered open to a world that was too bright. He screamed, but it was not in his usual voice. Instead, it was a high-pitch squeal. His arms flailed, and he noticed how pink and squishy they had become.

Am I... Am I a baby? He screamed again, protesting his situation. Around him, strange men and women, their faces covered in masks, moved him around.

"It's okay, Miguel," a woman's voice cooed, and warm hands took him from the strange, masked man.

He looked at the owner of the voice. She was an exhausted mess. Long strands of wet hair caked with sweat clung to her face.

Mother, he called, but all his body could muster was a confused grunt. For a split second, his anxiety fell away. The pain eased, and he took a tiny breath.

She gave a tired giggle, handing him away. *No, I don't want to go.*

A man's face filled Miguel's vision, and he squirmed in futile protest. He did not want this man; he wanted his mother.

"Miguel," he heard his mother say again. "It will be okay, child. It will be okay. Stay with daddy. Just for a little while."

Then the other people were screaming, saying something in that weird language. The man holding him looked concerned but gave him a reassuring bounce. He seemed to do what they were telling him, backing away from Miguel's mother. Miguel cried. He did not want this man, did not want to move away.

Something moved, something Miguel could not see. There were loud noises and yelling, lots of shouting. Miguel wanted to cry, so he did. He could cry whenever he wanted.

When he opened his mouth, tiny lungs filled with air, and Miguel screamed.

He screamed as the world fell away.

***

When his eyes fluttered open, Azul Maria was standing over him. “There, there, little one,” she whispered, helping him sit up. “Not too fast now. You took a nasty spill.”

With a ragged breath, he looked at Azul. “I need to get out of here.”

“No one goes back to the land of the living, Miguel.”

“I know, and I’m trying to move on. I … I need some air.”

“That I can help you with,” she whispered, guiding him back to his feet.

He tried to walk but tripped over his own feet. Azul caught him, righting him without effort. Together, they walked to the door, Miguel resting his arms on the frame.

“I saw my mother, myself being born. I would have been a father.” Tears ran down his face. “Why does it feel like death is following me?”

Azul Maria gave his shoulder a series of gentle squeezes. “Death is not following you, Mr. Miguel—no more than anyone else—and remember, you can see everyone again. Everyone has their Death Night Festival.”

“Then where is my mother?” he hissed with raw anger.

If he offended her, Azul made no show of it. Her face was an impassive mask. “Perhaps she’s already been here, or she’ll come later. It’s not my Death Night Festival, Mr. Miguel.”

“How do I leave this place?”

She pointed into the distance. “Keep going. You’ll see the light you want soon enough.”

“That’s it? Then why couldn’t I get out of here sooner?”

“Every child comes to my rooms looking for something. I believe you found what you needed.”

“Why would I want to know my son will grow up without a father or remember my mother dying?”

Azul shrugged, closing the door. “I said you had what you needed, not what you wanted, Mr. Miguel.”

Chapter 10: Violet Night

Stepping out onto a balcony, Miguel took a deep breath, enjoying the crisp air as it filled his aching lungs. A cool breeze brushed across him, and all his sharp pains faded, replaced with a general dull ache.

Here, he had a full view of the night sky, no longer restricted by the skylights in the game room. Comets raced across the sky, bright stars twinkled in the blackness of space, and then there was the moon. The moon was full and bigger than he had ever seen. He wondered how it was even possible for the universe to be so large. He walked to the rails, gazing up at the full night sky. Against that grandeur, he was so small, so insignificant and alone. *What chance do I have?*

Below him, cries of laughter and giggles of excitement came from one of the large in-ground pools. Everyone below was enjoying their night, oblivious to what was going on. *Would it be all right if I stopped here? Sit back, lean on this rail, and wait for the sun to come up. Can becoming a Lost One really be any worse?*

"Here I thought only Azul had her head in the clouds that much," Violeta Maria said, stepping out onto the balcony. She wore the same uniform as her sisters: white top, face paint, skirt colored to match her name, and headband. However, of the three Marias, Violeta was the best dressed. Every aspect of her appearance was crisp and form-fitted, and she carried herself with poise and confidence. If there was anything Violeta Maria had, it was confidence.

"Didn't Raquel tell you not to talk to me?" Miguel coughed. "I, uh, don't want you to get in trouble again because of me."

"Raquel might run the bar, but she doesn't control me. I will listen to her when she says something worth hearing. Otherwise, I talk to who I want, when I want." Violeta noticed the skeptical look on his face, "Plus, she said not to bother you *and* to do our jobs. Our jobs are helping people, which is what I'm doing right now." Stepping beside him, she scanned the sky. "So are you looking for astronomy reasons or just being pathetic?"

Miguel balked at the question; *most people* would ease into a question like that, but Violeta Maria was not *most people*. "If you must know, I was trying to decide what to do next."

"Ah." She sighed in mock enthusiasm. "Pathetic looking."

"It's not pathetic looking," he snapped back. "I'm considering my life and my afterlife. Neither one has panned out that well in case you hadn't noticed."

Violeta shrugged, kicking a loose piece of stone from the balcony and into the pool below.

"Don't do that," Miguel chastised.

"Why? The people down there can't see it, and it won't affect them. It's just a piece of rock, and I can fix it up with a thought." She tapped the spot where she'd found the loose stone, revealing the ledge to be restored.

"Because it isn't right. It's not what you should be doing."

She chuckled. "You say that, but you're the one still looking at the stars."

Miguel turned back up to the horizon. "It's more complicated than that. I've seen my past, remembered things."

"Death comes to everyone in time." She shrugged, not in apathy but in acceptance of something greater at play. "All we can do is make sure we are welcoming."

"Azul Maria had me hold a baby. When she took it back…" Miguel let out a breath, gathering his strength from the starry sky. "I remembered how I died. I was calling my wife. We would have had a party to announce we were having a baby boy. Then I panicked and passed out."

"The blue rooms have that effect on people," Violeta replied with a blunt laugh. "Although you may be the first to pass out. You must be a special person."

Ignoring her, Miguel continued. "Then I had a… dream? A flashback? I don't know, but I remembered my mother."

Violeta grunted in understanding. "I had the same reaction when she tried to make me hold one of those squirmy things, too. Well, without the memories of Madre. I mean, I can't remember what doesn't exist." She paused, and there was a sloshing sound. A moment later, a flask appeared in front of his face.

Muttering a thank-you, Miguel took a swig. Unlike the drink Raquel had served, which flowed into him and drew out a specific memory tied to his feelings, the flask's contents burned their way down, pulling out a multitude of memories all at once. The liquid ran down his throat, causing Miguel's entire life to flash before his eyes.

As his memories reached their end and he was stepping in front of Steven's car, the visions became jumbled. Sounds skipped like a record jumping tracks, and then the images tore like an old film reel. A blinding white light filled his mind, and then a new series began playing.

The new barrage of memories had a little girl running across a yard, chased by her father, who caught her with a growl and picked her up with a booming laugh. Then she was older, wearing braces and glasses, talking with other girls. A man walked by and said something that made her blush. The vision jumped again, and he was at her wedding. She wore a beautiful gown, standing before the altar with the man from earlier. He recognized the image from an old photograph. These were his parents. These were his mother's memories, her experiences and life. Their time together, their plans for him as they renovated the house, all the way until the moment of his birth. As the vision faded, his mother's words whispered into his mind, *It will be okay, Miguel.*

He swallowed, unsure how he was seeing his mother's memories. The act of swallowing, however, moved a little more of the potent liquid down his throat and fresh memories blazed to life in his mind. A boy, just born, held by Vanessa. A whole life ahead of him. The memories did not go any further, not because they reached an end, but because whatever vehicle was taking Miguel through these memories could not decide which path to follow. He heard a small laugh from the baby, and then Miguel snapped back to the moment.

Violeta laughed as he wiped hot tears running from his burning eyes; he could not speak, only push out his words like puffs of smoke. "What was all that? What's in that flask?"

"This is the pure stuff." She nodded, taking the flask and having a sip herself. "Straight from the source, before that lazy girl gets her ass out of bed each night. Direct joy from the source itself, no dilution." With a grunt under her breath, she added, "Raquel thinks she's so quick. Quick *only* helps when you're awake to stop me. Told you I'd get a taste of it one day."

"But what I saw? Those weren't just my memories. They were—"

"It's everything," she finished for him, taking another long drink. Unlike Miguel, she did not recoil from the liquid's burning sensation, but her speech was slurring. "The source is tapped into everyone. Raquel just gives you your portion. But I'm not Raquel." She gave him a wicked smile. "So you're welcome."

Exhilarated, he blew a few test breaths to see if fire would come from his mouth. He let out a giddy laugh, his nerves on high alert as every part of him tingled. He looked back at the sky and saw it all melt away. Everything smoothed back to where it would have been if he were alive. "This place is…" He trailed off, shaking his head. "It's amazing. It's so big, and…" He threw out his arms in a wide, exaggerated motion, trying to conjure more words. "It's just so big! I… I can't believe you all manage it each night, even if you are fast."

Violeta Maria shook her head, dismissing his compliment with her usual humility and grace. "I know, we are impressive. It's not our fault. We were made to be perfect. That's the burden I live with every night." She let out a giggle, and Miguel noticed the glazed look in her eyes from the flask. "But you know, this place used to be even bigger. Back in the early days, it was Los Cinco

Hermanas. The Five Sisters. *That* was when we had a festival to end all festivals, and we did it every night. Granted, *I* wasn't there, but I was still here, y'know. The shows, the games, the food. Such good times…"

"What happened?"

Violeta Maria shrugged. "The others left. One by one, they moved on. Happens in life, happens in death, I suppose. Running this place was fun, but we also had so many Lost Ones, too. More and more every night, and it broke the other sisters' hearts to see so many wanderings. When Muertos started handling it… they left. Everyone going out to find their own way, leaving just Muertos and her husband."

"Muertos is married?" he gasped.

Violeta laughed. "Why wouldn't she be?"

He was not sure what was more confusing about that statement: that a figure embodying death was married or that he thought it could be strange. "Who is her husband, then?"

"Death," Violeta replied, sounding a little sloppy. "You might not remember meeting him, but he brings everyone here." She grinned. "I wonder if he'd let me drive his car one day."

She rested her back on the rail, peering up with glazed eyes at the night sky. Whatever she was seeing was not in the stars above, but in something deep in her memories. “Things got bad…” She stopped, shaking her head and sliding her flask back into a sash around her waist. “Then Raquel came on full-time. It was bad enough when she came by for deliveries. But to have her here all the time?” Violeta leaned farther over the rails to spit in disdain, and Miguel reached out to draw her back onto the balcony before she fell over.

Taking the flask from her sash, he set it on the small table behind him. “You may have had enough, Violeta. This doesn’t taste like something anyone should drink.”

Ignoring him, she walked around the small area. “Raquel,” she grumbled. “Sure, she steps in, and everyone is happy. But did things get any better? No. That’s why *we’re* here.” Violeta pointed to herself to accent her point. “Bail her big butt out.”

“You don’t like her, do you?”

“Yeah, and what of it? I dislike people who keep secrets. She *butts*”—Violeta laughed at the word—“into our business but never lets us into hers.”

“You want her to let you run the bar?”

Violeta scoffed, making a growl like grinding rocks. “No, I don’t want to run the bar. The patio is bad enough.” Her wandering led her back to the railing, and Miguel prepared for another attempt at falling over. Instead, she gave him a wicked smile. “Although there are a lot of cuties out here…” Leaning, she peered over the balcony, letting out a sharp whistle that Miguel recognized all too well.

His face turned a shade redder, and he swore the temperature jumped several degrees.

Catching his reaction, she gave a chuckle and rose to her feet. “Yeah, it was me, but Lima also whistled. It’s just that humans can’t hear sounds that high-pitched.” She stalked over on unsteady legs and plopped down on the wicker couch. “Raquel’s problem is she won’t tell us about what comes next. We keep asking, but she won’t give up the details. She just shrugs and says”—Violeta mimicked Raquel’s voice, although her version of Raquel had a deep bass sound—“‘I can’t say, so stop asking. Don’t you have something better to do with your time? You’ll find out if you ever get there. Slow as you are, it’ll take you eternity.’”

He leaned back, surprised, repeating what she had said. “Raquel knows what comes next for us?”

Violeta opened her mouth to deliver a snippy answer but then stopped. While she was angry, something in his question made her pause. The swirling violet light in her eyes slowed, skipping a few beats, as she processed his comment. A few times she moved like she intended to respond but then thought again. “Of course she does. What are you? Dumb?”

There was no laughter in her tone, giving Miguel the impression that she was sobering up. “So what lets you and your sisters stay here so long?”

She rolled her eyes. “You don’t know? Raquel is right about one thing: humans are slow.” Miguel shrugged, having grown used to being insulted by this point, and Violeta let out a long, pained sigh. “We are spirits of this place.”

“So I’m talking to a house?”

"Do I *look* like a house to you?" Violeta Maria shouted while rising to her feet, her hands scaling up and down her frame to accent her point. "No, my sisters and I are manifestations of this location, this *time* in a person's death. We're supposed to bring comfort, joy, and acceptance. It's just… ever since Muertos figured out how to *resolve* the Lost Ones, things have been… more intense."

Miguel nodded. Even the best of features would bend under enough stress and pressure. If Azul was a comforter, then pushing that too far would become laziness. Lima's need to spread joy had given her continual anxiety. That would leave Violeta in the role of acceptance, but if Raquel were keeping something as big as the afterlife from her, well, Miguel could see her frustration. "Well, you're the best-looking house spirits I've ever seen. I also think you do a fine job here."

For a moment, she gawked at him, stunned. Miguel thought about raising his hands in case she smacked him but leaned back a little in his seat just in case.

Violeta said nothing. The face paint hid most of her face, but Miguel could have sworn he saw a slight blush even through the white makeup.

She did her best to avoid meeting Miguel's eyes. "Anyway, Raquel says she can't tell us what's on the other side because she doesn't know, but…" She pursed her lips until they were a faint line. "But I'm sure she knows something. I just need to open up. I will one day, you know. Angel or not, I'm sure I can get her to talk."

"Would Raquel lie to you?"

"Angels don't lie. At least none of the Good Ones would."

"Is Raquel a Good One? I mean, she's here, isn't she?"

Violeta Maria's mouth hung open in shocked horror at the accusation. She opened her mouth to reply, then stopped. Drawing up to her full height, which wouldn't have been taller than Miguel, had he been standing, she pointed a violet fingernail at him. "Let me be *perfectly* clear about something, Mr. Miguel. Raquel del Fuego is a pain in the ass on every conceivable level. She finds fresh ways to be obnoxious, rude, and infuriating every day. *This* I know from personal experience." She waved her finger in front of him, reminding Miguel of a cobra ready to strike. "But she *is* one of the Good Ones. Never speak ill of her."

"Then perhaps she doesn't know what comes next," he replied. "It's possible no one does until it's time."

Violeta looked deflated and backed away. He was glad to no longer have her in his face, but he shared her disappointment. Miguel kind of wanted to be wrong so he could get Raquel to tell him what awaited them after this. "Maybe…" She mulled the word over, then turned to look over the rail at the people splashing in the water below.

"Maybe," he repeated.

"You know…" Violeta laughed, moving a few strands of hair from her face. "When I saw you run from the children's hall"—Miguel winced, not liking how weak that made him sound—"I thought, *Oh no, Maria, he'll go puking on a balcony, and you know Azul and Lima won't see it. Better go before it gets worse.*" She nodded at him. "But in the end, I feel I got the most from this talk. Thank you, Mr. Miguel."

He laughed. "Or you wanted a reason to get drunk where no one could see you and I was a good excuse."

Violeta grinned. "It could be many things. As you said, 'the unknown path ahead.'" She looked around, then leaned in, planting a quick kiss on his cheek. "For luck. You may need it."

“My pleasure,” he said, then turned back toward the principal building. “I have had enough air. It’s time to go back inside. Time to see where the night will take me. Since this is my last night, I may as well enjoy it. No sense in holding back.”

“That’s the spirit.” Violeta laughed, accenting the last word with a grin. “Let me know if you need anything tonight. I might be willing to run something to you.” She patted the spot where she had tucked her flask. “Or if you just need a little more clarity.” In a purple blur of motion, Violeta Maria vanished, leaving Miguel alone on the balcony.

He took one last deep breath of cool night air, then strode back in, determined to see tonight through.

Chapter 11: Closing Out the Bar

Stepping out of the back rooms, Miguel braced himself for the experience. The recreational areas had been quiet and set aside, allowing him the time he needed to process some of what he had been going through. Now, back in the main hall, music blared, people danced, and voices rang out. It all hit him at once, but Miguel had found a focus, and this time, it did not knock him off his feet.

His focus, Juan Pedro, was on the stage, playing and moving like there was no tomorrow. Miguel scratched his head. Was there a tomorrow here or would it always be tonight? *Just someone else's tonight, I suppose.* Rubbing the bridge of his nose, Miguel tried not to think too much about how time worked here.

Back to business, he declared, steeling himself before plunging into the crowds once more. The dance floor had become pure chaos, as groups of people occupied the same space, but no one collided. Arms swung through bodies without harm as each person's Death Night Festival went off in its own way. Tiny worlds colliding with no one any the wiser for it.

After the night he had experienced, Miguel walked forward into the maelstrom of parties. He had no intent on joining in with any group and focused on the stage. Stepping through people still sent a twinge down his spine, but when he reached the stage without injury, he allowed himself a smile. *No harm done.*

As he completed his self-assessment, ensuring everything was still there, and no more bruised than it had been before, Juan Pedro appeared above him. With the bandleader no longer in his spot, the music became less pronounced. Notes lost their crispness, and the melody became unfocused, but the rhythm seemed to stay the same. To anyone else, it might have been easy to miss, but Miguel had been hearing the music since opening, and he could tell when Juan Pedro was not center stage.

The music is off-key, he noted. *Was that what Raquel heard last night?* Miguel laughed, wondering when he started noticing changes in music.

Greeting him with a quick handshake, a wide grin, and an appreciative chuckle, Juan Pedro rendezvoused to meet Miguel at the stage's stairs. "Miguel! Are you ready to join me? I told you I would hold you to your promise. Now you are here." In his free hand, Juan Pedro held out a small guitar sized more for a child than a man. A simple wooden instrument, it was not as elegant as those being used by the band.

"I can't play," Miguel reminded Juan Pedro. "I haven't strummed a guitar since my wedding, and that was because my brother-in-law played for me. I wasn't even that good at pretending, and I don't think I could play a tune to save my life."

"Then it is a good thing your life can no longer be on the line." Juan Pedro laughed, placing a hand on Miguel's shoulder to pull him upward. "Come," he said with a brilliant smile. "Come join your friend on the stage. I promise you, tonight will be one you shall never forget."

Miguel shook his head, wanting nothing more than to offer a kind rejection and melt back into the crowds. That all changed when he saw the eagerness in Juan Pedro's eyes and heard the excitement in his voice. *You can do this*, a voice whispered from deep inside. With butterflies in his stomach, he reached out to take the offered hand, and within a few quick steps, Miguel found himself on stage.

"Everyone! Everyone!" Juan Pedro roared into the microphone, holding up a hand to signal the crowd. Dancing stopped and cries of joy went silent as a sea of faces watched Miguel. The band swarmed around Miguel with rapid precision, setting up a microphone, fitting the small guitar with a shoulder strap, and making subtle modifications to Miguel's posture. Their movements were so quick he wondered if they were spirits of the house, like the Marias. After a flurry of motion, straps being tweaked and cords being plugged into equipment, Miguel appeared to belong on the stage, at least from a technical perspective.

Miguel's clothes, a plain polo, khakis, and brown shoes, stood in stark contrast to those of the band. Everyone was wearing dark blue suits, matching ties and hats, and hot pink dress shirts.

"Time to get changed, Miguel," the band member making his final adjustments said. "You're one of us now, and we have an image to maintain." The man's smile was kind but insistent.

"Haven't you got him ready yet, Enrique?" another band member chided.

Enrique cast the heckler a casual shrug while rolling his head toward Miguel. "Showtime, Miguel."

Miguel swallowed, then sputtered out a reply. "You want me to change here? Now? I don't know if you know this, but the last time I tried something with clothes, I ended up—"

"Naked? Yes, we saw that from the stage. Hilarious, and a bold move when talking with a señorita, but I wouldn't advise you do that *this* time." He gave Miguel a grin and a wink. "We rarely play *that* kind of show."

Juan Pedro continued speaking to the crowd while Miguel fought to untie his stomach knots. Panic filled him. This would differ from imagining a pad of paper or anything else he had created tonight. This was magically changing his clothes in front of an uncountable number of people. *Okay, focus on changing clothes.* He closed his eyes, breathing in slow breaths. *Remember what*

Juan Pedro is wearing. I just need to be wearing that.

When he opened his eyes, nothing had changed. *I can't. I can't imagine how I'd look in their uniforms. It's not my style.*

Shutting his eyes again, he squeezed them together. *Okay, don't focus on the clothes. Maybe just think about being in the band. I want to be in the band.*

Even through clenched eyes, Miguel could feel the crowd's attention upon him. *I'm a part of their celebration now. Please, let me be dressed.* For a moment, he saw the band attire in his mind and then panicked as he opened his eyes. The spotlight shining into his eyes, one last thought whispered, *Please don't let me be naked.* His eyes shot open, and he looked down, hopeful. *Not naked, but not changed.*

Juan Pedro's voice roared high. "Tonight, we have someone special joining us on stage. He just arrived this very night and is here for one night only!"

Miguel's mind whirled. He wondered if he could move quickly enough to fall off the back of the stage and flee out of the revealing spotlight, back into obscurity. Even being in the blue rooms again might be a blessing.

The bandleader's introduction continued. "So please, help me give a festive welcome to the one…"

Casting his eyes over the crowd, looking for any distraction, the guitar slipped in his sweaty palms.

He fought down the urge to throw up by shutting his eyes. *It's no use. I'm no musician. I told Juan Pedro I haven't played since my wedding, and that was all staged. My brother-in-law did all the playing. I just pretended, looking at Vanessa for a cue to leave.*

"… the only…" Juan Pedro continued, rising to his feet to point over at Miguel.

Vanessa. His wife's image came to mind. He saw her at the table. She looked equal parts concerned and proud as her husband stood shaking on the stage. She laughed, and he had always remembered her laughing with him, not at him.

The knots in his stomach loosened, and Miguel allowed himself a small smile. *I played for her that night. That night I was in the band. Tonight I can be again.* With a long exhale, he opened his eyes.

"… Miguel!" Juan Pedro finished his introduction, and the crowd matched the bandleader's exuberant energy, screaming and clapping as the spotlights whirled upon him.

Miguel smiled back at the crowd, reveling because he was, in fact, not naked, but dressed to match the others on stage. His clothes weren't as neat and pressed, but they matched, and he was not naked before an army of strangers.

Juan Pedro gave an exaggerated nod so even those in the back of the hall could see the motion. The crowd settled, going from a dull roar to murmurs of excitement. "Now, Miguel says he doesn't play. But I say—*we all* say—that music is one part the physical and the rest the soul." The crowd clapped in agreement. "So, *Miguel*, let us hear you play!"

This is it. Miguel gulped and, with a powerful motion, thrust his hand at the strings, attempting to mimic what he remembered seeing others do.

Intention and reality did not always walk arm in arm.

As his shoulder moved, the clip holding the guitar in place snapped free, and the neck swung down to smack him in the leg. Miguel let out a yelp in surprise.

"Well, music *is* one part physical," Enrique said into his microphone, getting a laugh from the audience while Miguel recovered. The crowd seemed to regard Miguel's failure as a part of the show, and despite his embarrassment, Miguel laughed. With a bow of his head, he waved an apology.

The knots in his stomach released a little more as he realized the night would continue despite his mistake; he had ruined nothing. Miguel flashed back to his last time on stage when people laughed but clapped along. *We're all here to enjoy tonight. Keep moving and it will be all right.* Juan Pedro, Enrique, and the rest knew how to keep the atmosphere light and people laughing, they were masters of entertaining crowds and they were bringing him along as one of their own. He could see he was among friends, and things would be okay.

Juan Pedro motioned for Miguel to come stand next to him and made a show of putting Miguel's hands in the proper places. "There. Much better," he said with a satisfied grin for the crowd. "Good."

Miguel nodded.

"Such a talker." Juan Pedro laughed, drawing more laughter from the crowd.

Miguel leaned into the microphone. “Perhaps, Juan Pedro, we should get back to playing.” There was a cacophony of approval from the audience, and the bandleader held up his hands in mock surrender.

There was a loud count to four, and the band roared to life. The sudden power and volume of the music shook Miguel in his spot, and the momentum continued to grow as time passed. Miguel looked to each band member, trying to mimic his dancing and the way Juan Pedro played. Occasionally, he reached over to make an adjustment to Miguel’s hands or whisper a word of instruction under his breath.

They played into the night, song after song, changing styles and speed, but never stopping. When he knew the words, Miguel sang along, but otherwise, he provided backup. Nothing he did was extraordinary or would ever win him any contest, but he was doing it, and he was having fun.

Time flew by as Miguel surrendered himself to the music, dancing, and performing. In the heart of all that chaos, he thought back to the night's beginning. *When we first met, all I wanted was to get away from him. Now look at me, sharing a stage with Juan Pedro.*

The excitement of that thought washed over him but did not last long. The band was in constant motion. He focused on keeping pace, but just when found his rhythm, the energy of the moment had moved on and Miguel struggled to meet the new rhythm.

With one final explosive barrage, it all ended. There was a roar from the crowd, and applause thundered like a storm. Miguel looked up, confused, unsure what he should do as Juan Pedro made a show of thanking each member of his crew.

There are so few left. The few remaining people no longer danced or screamed with joy. They listened to Juan Pedro's closing remarks, and one by one, they disappeared. Without the crowd, Miguel could see how the room had changed; it had returned to the wedding reception he remembered from earlier. The overhead lights had dimmed, leaving only the tabletop candles for light. A staggering, exhaustive wave hit him as he tried to determine how long he had been up there. Originally, he meant to play one or two songs, enough to honor his commitment, but soon, he found himself drawn into the allure of the stage.

"Juan Pedro," Miguel gasped in a ragged breath. Even though he had been doing simple chords, it had drained him of every drop of his reserve energy.

"How do you do this every night? I'm exhausted!" As he shook his head, beads of sweat flew from Miguel's mop of soaked hair. "In fact, *why* do you do this every night? I thought spirits did this one night, then moved on."

"Ah, yes." He sighed before pulling out his large handkerchief to wipe the sweat from his brow. "Well, it is a tale, amigo. I've always wanted to be a musician and play to a crowd."

Miguel's smile faded a shade. "But you're a brilliant musician and you seem to be a good man. Wouldn't heaven be the greatest stage?"

"No." Juan Pedro nodded. "No, heaven for me would not be a crowd. Besides, would it be real, or would it just be what I wanted *my* heaven to include?"

Miguel said nothing, searching for a place to set down his guitar. While everything else in the bar had a place, he could not find a stand or case for the small guitar. He turned to ask where he should put the instrument, but the look on Juan Pedro's face gave him pause. While they met that night, Miguel had only ever seen Juan Pedro carry himself with confidence and energy, a larger-than-life personality eager for anything the night provided. In this quiet moment, the musician seemed diminished.

"What makes you say that?" Miguel asked.

Juan Pedro reached over with care and took the small guitar from Miguel. He turned it over in his hands, examining it as if he had not seen it in years. "You see, when I was a young man, about your age…" He paused, examining Miguel for a moment. "I was better dressed and much better looking," he quipped before continuing. "I dreamed of being a musician."

Juan Pedro gazed into the sole spotlight, appearing to see something in that bright white light. A smile creased his broad face. "Oh, how I loved to play. Even then." Tearing his eyes away, he strummed the small guitar a few times, making some adjustments before repeating the motion. "I went out *every* night, playing one gig after another. Sometimes I was a hit. Often I was a flop."

Chuckling with enough force to make his belly shake, Juan played a series of energetic chords as if in response to what he was seeing in his mind. "To be fair, I was more often a flop than not."

Miguel swallowed and came to stand between Juan Pedro and the blinding spotlight. His shadow fell over the musician. "What happened?"

"The same thing that happens to many a musician. I went home broke."

"And then?"

He nodded. "And then… then I would play for my little sister. *Every* night she would come up to me when I came home." His voice changed, becoming a rather good replica of a little girl's voice. "'Juan Pedro! Juan Pedro! Play for me, big brother! I want to hear the world's greatest musician.'" He swallowed, letting his voice return to his normal growl. "I would, of course, oblige her."

Juan Pedro played a cheerful tune for a few moments, tapping his foot as he did so. When he stopped, he looked at Miguel with somber eyes. "She would tell me…" He stopped, gulping down a thought. "She would tell me she knew I would be the biggest star and that she would be there when I played before my largest crowd. I would always promise her that one day I would make that dream a reality for both of us."

Miguel moved to speak but found that the words had caught in his throat.

"But then I died. I don't know how it happened, but like everyone else, I came here. Food, drink, dance, and, of course, music. I played with the band, and it was the greatest feeling I had ever known. Yet despite all that, something was missing. Something was preventing me from genuinely enjoying the night."

“Your sister,” Miguel answered.

“Si.” He nodded. “It wasn’t enough. I could not move on. As grand as this festival had been, it was not enough. It was not how I would end *my* night. So I approached Madame Muertos.”

“She let you stay on. I thought everyone had to pass from here by daybreak?”

Juan Pedro’s face shifted, growing cold and hard. He winced as he spoke. “Not everyone. No, not everyone. Some become lost. But that is not for me, amigo. No, we made a deal. She allows me to stay on and lead the band until I can see my sister again.”

“But why? When you could move on and see her in the next life? Why wait for her here?”

“It’s simple.” At this, he stood up and placed the guitar in a case that had been in his shadow. He reached out, pulling Miguel into a gentle headlock, waving his hand to paint a picture of his vision. “I told Muertos when the day arrives that she comes here, I must be here. I will play music as my sister has never heard before, lead the band, and perform before the grandest crowd ever.” Juan Pedro drew in a deep breath to steady himself. “She will get to see me, Juan Pedro, fulfilling my promise. She will see me center stage, at the peak of my glory." They stood together for a moment, nodding at the shared mental image. "At the end of the night, my sister will then look at me, as eager and excited as when she was just a little girl. She will ask me"—he changed his voice back to an imitation of his sister—"'Brother, please! Please play for me again! I want to hear you. I want to hear the world's *greatest* musician!'" He cleared his throat, returning to his normal voice. "I will look her in the eyes, and do you know what I will say, Miguel?"

Miguel considered the question but could not think of anything that could mirror the gravity of the moment Juan Pedro had described. "No," he whispered, his own voice cracking.

"I will say, 'Of course I will, Mija.'" He placed a hand on his chest, pushing down on his heart with fierce determination. "I will play for you Juan more time."

Silence hung for a long moment.

Juan Pedro gave a faint chuckle before breaking into a deep, soulful laugh that shook his entire body. He clapped Miguel on the back, and the younger man found himself caught up in the laughter.

When his sides stopped hurting, Miguel held up a hand. "You're telling me you're waiting all this time *just* to make a terrible pun?"

"Not *all* of time, and not *just* to make a terrible pun. No, I wait for the *right* time to make the *best* pun of a lifetime."

Behind them, a throat cleared. Raquel stood with her usual dour expression and a drink for each of them. "Last call for drinks. Figured you'd want something after all that jumping around."

"Ah, such service!" Juan Pedro smirked, taking the glass and nodding to Miguel to do the same. "Thank you. I knew you were warming up to me, Raquel."

"Juan tell you his lame joke?" Raquel asked, rolling her eyes at the bandleader.

"Everyone is a critic," the musician complained with a smile. "They do not appreciate true genius in its time. At least the lady of the house can see that." He took a small sip from his glass, savoring each drop. "You know, if she didn't pour the—"

"Yeah, yeah, we know," Raquel interrupted. "I might have eternity, but I don't have that much time to hear the same joke over and over. After all this time, you'd think you'd learn *at least one* new joke."

Still elated from his stage performance and a little giddy from laughing, Miguel gave her a gentle tap on the arm, meant to be a kind gesture. "It's all in the spirit of moving on, right? Everyone needs help sometimes. I mean, that's what Violeta said."

At the name, Raquel lifted an eyebrow as she looked at her arm. "Miguel, do you remember why I'm here?" She cracked her knuckles in a casual motion, never taking her eyes off him.

Miguel heard her words in his mind. *I don't like being touched. I responded in kind.* "Ah," he got out before adding a quick apology. Raquel nodded. Then her scowl broke, and she let out the most obnoxious sound Miguel had ever heard. *Is that a laugh?*

He turned to Juan Pedro, who mirrored his confusion.

Before either could speak, Raquel slapped his arm, causing him to wince as stars filled his vision. She had avoided the arm that held his drink, but his entire frame still shook. *Well, she didn't hit me. That's probably as close to jovial as Raquel will get.*

“Oh, man!” she gasped. “You should see that stupid look on your face.” With a loud snort, she straightened up, then pointed at him. “Yeah, just like that.”

Miguel groaned. Raquel’s version of humor left something to be desired, especially if you were on the receiving end of it. “Yeah,” he whimpered in a high-pitched voice. “You got me.”

With a wave, she walked from the stage.

“Well, now that’s something you don’t see every day. I think she may like you, amigo.” Juan Pedro elbowed him in the ribs. Miguel was thankful that the musician had avoided his arm. “Even Enrique can’t get her to smile at him, and he’s the lady’s man.”

“What can I say? It’s true,” Enrique shouted back as he packed up the stage. “Ladies love me, and I can’t say I blame them.” The others groaned at his comment but otherwise paid him no mind as they finalized packing up their equipment.

Miguel coughed, taking a sip of his drink as sensation came back to his arm. *If that means she likes me, I'm* glad *she isn't angry at me. Still…* He looked at his sore arm. *Will that leave a bruise? Can the dead still bruise?* Deciding not to think about himself for what little time he had left with Juan Pedro, he turned to the larger man. "Speaking of Enrique, was he with you? Are all the band members here on a similar loan? You all seem to play well together."

"Their story is too long to tell tonight. Another time, perhaps?" Juan Pedro nodded. "Best to say they are on loan for a time. A sort of credit situation."

"Okay then, Juan Pedro, one more question. It's something I've been wondering about all night."

"I do not give autographs. Part of my contract, you understand. I have to make sure my brand stays pure."

"No," Miguel continued without pause; when talking to Juan Pedro, it was best to ignore the comments and stay on topic. "I was wondering, what do you think of Muertos? Do you think she looks—"

"Beautiful?" Juan Pedro interjected before shouting, "Hey, Enrique, Miguel's after Muertos, too."

"Aw, come on, man!" Enrique shouted back, placing his hands over his heart. "Isn't one señorita enough? Must you mock your friend Enrique by having them *all* to yourself?"

"No, that's not…" Flustered, Miguel downed the last of his drink for a shot of happy courage. "I wanted to know if you find her familiar."

The smile on the bandleader's face faded. "Well, she is our boss. So yes."

"You don't think you knew her before you came here?"

Both shook their heads. Enrique opened his mouth to continue the jokes, but Juan Pedro held up a hand, showing that, for once, now was not the time.

"I'm sorry, my friend, but no. If you do… well, I don't know if you are lucky to have known her before or if that is an omen. You would be the first person I've met that knew her before they got here. Even most people who are here never meet Madame Muertos." Patting his legs, Juan Pedro rose to his feet. "I am unsure what you were hoping I could tell you, but I must thank you for playing with us tonight. No matter what comes next for you, I hope we have another chance to play together."

"Juan more time," Miguel offered, taking his hand.

"Leave the jokes to the professionals," Juan Pedro growled. Somewhere, Miguel thought he could hear Raquel scoff.

"I'm afraid it doesn't look good for me. I may have wasted the night. Closing time is coming up quickly."

Releasing Miguel's hand, Juan Pedro shook a finger at him. "Remember what I told you when we first met?"

"That I was jumpy?"

"No, I told you not to waste your time on such deep thoughts. You should stay in the here and now and enjoy all the night has to offer."

“You said all that to distract me and steal my drink,” Miguel countered.

Juan Pedro laughed back. “Think of this, and take care, amigo.”

Miguel shook his head, looking out at the vacant room. When he turned back, Juan Pedro had gone. A pang of sadness hit him in the gut, and he stepped off the empty stage. The spotlight went off with a loud click, and Miguel made his clothes return to his normal attire. It felt wrong to be on stage without Juan Pedro and even worse to wear his style of clothing when he was alone, as if he were stealing something by imitating the bandleader.

As he reached the last step, he saw Madame Muertos at the bar with Raquel and the Marias. Based on the employees' expressions and postures, it seemed Muertos was going over the night's activities and providing feedback. Looking at Violeta's and Raquel's reactions, Miguel guessed that it must have fallen in the “areas for improvement” category.

Weariness filled his limbs as he plopped himself down at one of a dozen remaining tables. He wanted nothing more than to sit and rest, and this might be his last chance.

Morning would be here soon, and since he had not moved on, he would soon become one of the Lost Ones.

Chapter 12: One of the Lost Ones

With Juan Pedro's band no longer playing, Madame Muertos's home was an eerie place. Everything remained decorated for a party, but there was no need for the spotlights on stage, leaving the room illuminated by the bar's backlighting and the small, colorful candles on each table.

Miguel produced a piece of paper and wrote notes in the dim light. When he met Madame Muertos again, he hoped to have all his thoughts in order, to show her what he had done and prove he was worthy of moving on.

A woman cleared her throat, startling Miguel. When he lifted his head, he jumped again.

What appeared to be a young woman sat at this table, giving him an angry, withering look. She was a tall, lean figure that glowed with a silver-blue color. *A Lost One.* A chill ran through his veins. *That's what I thought I was seeing all night. They have been stalking me.*

Glancing back to Raquel's counter, Miguel prepared to call out for the bartender's help. However, the bar's lights were out, the Marias, Raquel, and Muertos nowhere in sight.

"Did you *want* something?" she snapped. There was pain in her voice, and frozen tears glistened at the corners of her eyes. The woman seemed ready to break at any moment, and Miguel feared he might be the one to push her over the edge. While he had heard nothing about the Lost Ones being violent, he did not want to learn. She clenched the table, one hand holding a napkin in a vise-like grip while the other squeezed the air. Whatever events had led her here tonight, it had not been a simple road to travel.

Averting his eyes, Miguel struggled to say something to put her at ease. "I'm sorry. I did not mean to intrude. I didn't see you here."

"No, popular people like you never do."

Miguel reeled as if he had been struck, his mouth cracking into a goofy smile. A weak laugh slipped out. "I'm sorry. It is just no one has ever called me that before tonight. What makes you think I'm popular?"

She regarded him with a tight sneer, shifting her shoulders at his challenge. Then she nodded to the stage. "You were up there with the band. I saw you playing. We all did."

"We all did," he repeated, slowly turning to see Lost Ones surrounding him. Some stood in the space between tables, while others sat alone. Unlike the regular tables, there was no food or drink on them, only a single candle with a pale flame that remained motionless. Each of the Lost Ones wore the same tense expression as the woman in front of him, and all of them glowed with the same silver-blue color. More Lost Ones continued to drift in from parts unknown, standing away from the other tables but always edging closer to watch Miguel.

As more of them gathered, they illuminated the room in silver-blue light that twisted everything it touched. The stage appeared gaunt and warped, its flooring shifting into a snarl like some magnificent beast. Tables were lopsided and unstable in the glow, and bottles at Raquel's bar looked broken, like someone had placed shattered glass on its shelves. Everything gave off an oppressive aura of defeat and hopelessness.

The Morose.

"You even drank with the musician." She swallowed with dry disdain.

Cold sweat formed on his brow. Her words tore into him, as if he were on trial. Looking to the gathered Lost Ones, Miguel soon understood that was a genuine possibility. What would they do to him if his answers were not to their liking? Could they hurt him? Would that be their version of having a festival?

"No, you see, I was just standing nearby. He wanted me to play the guitar. I didn't do much, just followed instructions. You saw I wasn't particularly good. Besides, I couldn't have said no. Juan Pedro is just… warm."

The woman shivered at the word, cold ice in her eyes. "Well, you were talking with the bartender all night."

"Raquel? She told me to keep checking in with her. She… Well, she scares me. I wouldn't say no to her… ever."

Her eyes squinted to a glare. "You seem to have an 'in' with her and the staff. Do you work here?"

"Look." Miguel exhaled, raising his hands before him. "I don't want any trouble from you. I'm here just like everyone else."

A joyless smile crossed her lips. “You are nothing like the rest of us.”

“I’m nothing special,” he countered. Something about her, or perhaps the aura she was giving off, repulsed him. *Just stand up and turn away from her. From all of them. Get out of here and find Raquel or Muertos. Perhaps the Marias can help.*

“Go then,” she spat. “Get up and walk away.”

As Miguel rose, he reached for his papers, the words *when to speak* catching his eye. This would be the first and last time he would see this woman, and while he didn’t want to fight with her or spend what little time he had left being attacked, Miguel also did not want to brush her off. Whoever she was, she looked troubled. *Haven’t people been helping me all night? I should try to return the favor. Besides, where else can I go?*

“The only difference between me and anyone else is I got here before the bar opened. That’s it. If anyone is talking to me, it’s because that is apparently weird.”

She scoffed. All around, the other Lost Ones mirrored her reaction. “So you ate and drank with strangers because you got here early? You think you can do whatever you want without consequences?”

“No,” he countered. “I tried my best to enjoy tonight. I had a few drinks, some cake, a coffee, that sort of thing. Food wasn’t a priority.” Miguel held the last syllable longer than he should have. Looking at the gaunt woman, he wondered when she last had a good meal. Then he wondered when he had last eaten.

“I was out for lunch before it all happened,” Miguel muttered to himself, and his stomach growled. “I apologize, but I could go for something to eat. Would you care to join me? Perhaps we could split a platter of something. Maybe some desserts.”

She said nothing and made no move, as if what he said had not even registered, only watching him with those ready-to-burst eyes.

A large white plate clacked down in front of him. Unfortunately, it was not a platter, as he had hoped, only one single item and a piece of folded paper.

Written in tiny, neat handwriting upon it were the words, *Kitchen was closed for a private event. Not much left. Grabbed what I could.* It was signed by Violeta.

Miguel turned the note over, a bemused look on his face. *Figures that I would be too late to order my own last meal...*

Turning his attention to what Violeta had brought out, he found his companion leaning forward to examine the new arrival. Until now, the most the Lost One had moved would have been to twist her head from side to side and to wring her napkin. Her frozen posture and silver-blue glow had added to the otherworldly appearance. Seeing her loom closer sent a chill down Miguel's spine.

"Is that a churro?" She gulped, her eyes shifting to the plate. The woman reached out and took it before Miguel could protest. Her hand shook, sending cinnamon and sugar cascading onto the table below. The fallen spices twinkled in the pale light, adding an infinitesimal speck of color to the landscape. "It is." She sighed, turning the dessert in her hand with care. "I remember these. My grandma used to call me her little churro."

The lean woman straightened in her seat, her face contorting into a stern expression, and her voice was a raspy cough. "Izabella, my little churro," she said to no one. It sounded as if she were mimicking someone older. "Do you know why I call you this?"

She paused, her voice changing again, this time sounding younger. "No, Grandma," she answered herself.

"Because you are so tall and so s-sweet…" She stopped, her impression breaking as the tears started cascading down her silver-blue cheek. Miguel could make out a faint trail of color in their wake, a fleshy tone under the silver-blue glow, as if the pain in those tears was washing away the aura. After a few seconds to collect her voice, Izabella forced herself to continue. "You are so tall and so sweet to me…" Her voice broke again. She clenched her fist around the churro, smashing it in her vise-like grip. As she raised her hands to her eyes, Miguel grabbed her fallen napkin and replaced it in her hands before she could smear her eyes with churro.

Seeing the napkin, she traded it to Miguel for the dessert and wiped her face. Her voice took on a new tone, no longer frozen and far off. She sounded human, with a genuine sadness in her words. As Izabella spoke, she appraised herself. “I’m such a mess. If she saw me now, she’d be so ashamed.”

“Izabella,” he whispered, happy to have Izabella with him instead of a creature. Somehow that thought made the surrounding chill lessen, if only a little. Now he was talking to *someone.* Looking her over, he wondered if she would be okay. She still gave off the silver-blue glow like the other Lost Ones, but she seemed different now. Izabella looked focused, as if she belonged fully in the room instead of being a lingering apparition.

He thought back to the woman in his office, how he had said the wrong thing and she ran out in tears. *What did I say that was so bad?* Miguel focused on that moment, and the memory came surging forward, striking with the force of a cannonball.

The woman had been in Miguel's office many times, and they had talked for long periods. She had come in trying to make an appointment, and he had to refuse her. "I'm too busy right now. Perhaps tomorrow?" Then she left his office. *I never saw her again. No one did.* Looking at the throng of Lost Ones, Miguel wondered if she had been here, too. If that woman was here because of him.

"Izabella," he said again, this time loud enough for her to hear. The Lost One turned, looking at him from behind a face streaked with tears. He paused, mulling over the words in his head, trying to find the perfect thing he could say to help. Everything that came to mind seemed wrong or too clichéd. Instead, he shook his head. "I don't know what to say. I can't speak for you or your grandmother." She recoiled. "What I can tell you is this: I spent the entire night here trying to figure out what makes me special, to find a purpose, a reason to move on. In the end, all I did was talk to people, and it made me remember how much I missed those I care about. How I would do anything in the world to see them again." He paused, meeting her gaze. "If I were your grandmother, then I know I would love nothing more than to see you."

"Why?" she asked, confused, tears now rushing down her face. "Why would you say that?" With a deep, pained swallow, she tried in vain to dry her cheeks. Words stuck in her throat, and she had to cough to get them out. "Why would… Why would she still want me? I was so bad. I screwed up. I made her cry."

He looked at the ruined dessert on the table between them. It was mashed and torn to pieces, cinnamon-scented mush, but Miguel smiled and took a bite. Then he held up the remaining pieces to her. "Even a *screwed-up* churro is delicious."

She laughed, but not with the cold dismissal she had before. A change had come over her, a slight change to be sure, but Izabella's laugh had a bit of warmth to it. "You are crazy," she said. "It's ruined. It can't be any good."

"Try it and see," he replied. "I have it on good authority that only the finest food is served here."

She picked over the churro's ruins, finding a sizeable piece that was still recognizable, closed her eyes, and took a bite. When her eyes opened, they were brown, no longer the silver-blue color the other Lost Ones possessed. She nodded her approval. "You're right. It's exactly like grandma used to make."

Miguel chuckled, relief washing over him. Izabella laughed, still dabbing at her eyes but now with less intensity.

On the table in front of him, the candle flickered. While the light was still pale, it was moving.

"What am I doing here?" Izabella wondered aloud. "I should be looking for Grandmama, maybe give her a call." Reaching to the floor, she picked up a purse and rummaged through its contents until she found her phone. "Ugh! No bars. How—"

An explosive force struck the front door, causing them both to jump. The blow came again and again, each strike sounding more powerful than the last.

Nothing opens that door unless it's meant to, Miguel tried to reassure himself before sliding his chair back. The attack stopped, and silence hung for a tense moment. *What would dare attack Madame Muertos's home?*

Muertos appeared, stepping out of whichever shadows she existed in between moments, and regarded the door with a tense stare. Something strained against the door, no longer hitting it but shifting to a constant pressure. Then, with a final mighty heave by whatever was outside, the door opened with a thunderous boom.

Muertos stepped forward, placing herself between them and the invader.

What stepped inside was not a monster, a demon, or a nightmarish ghoul. Instead, in walked a frail old woman. She propped herself up on a firm wooden cane. She scanned the room through her thick gold-rimmed glasses. After a few turns of her head, she focused on Madame Muertos. “Eh! You there! Señorita! Are you the one responsible for this?”

Muertos smiled, making an awkward bow on her last few steps to the door. “Yes, Madame. How can I help you?”

“Here!” the old woman roared, raising her cane. “What’s the meaning of locking me out?”

“Uh, the door was not locked.” Madame Muertos coughed. “Sometimes the door… sticks. At least for some.”

“Then you need to grease it, fix it, something! It was stuck so badly I almost couldn’t get it open. Don’t you know I’m here to see someone? I didn’t come all this way to be kept out by a faulty door. Honestly, I thought this place used to be run properly.”

"I'm sorry, but…" Muertos giggled, trying to defuse the woman's anger. For the first time that night, Miguel thought Muertos looked taken aback. It was strange to see their hostess so out of sorts when talking to anyone. "But since you *are* inside now, can I help you? A drink? Something to eat? We are about to close for the day, but—"

"But, but, but," the older woman chastised. "Too much 'but' with señoritas these days. Stop with the buts. I'm here for…" The old lady stopped. Her cane clattered to the floor, and the broadest of toothless grins Miguel had ever seen formed across her face.

"Izabella!" she shouted. "Is that you, my little churro?"

"Grandmama!" Izabella replied in kind, racing from the table and toward the old woman. Izabella wrapped her elder in a vise-like hug. "How did you find me?"

"Little churro," the grandmother clucked. "I can always find you."

Miguel looked away, not wanting to intrude on their reunion. As he did, something caught his attention. The silver-blue aura had left Izabella as she hugged her grandmother. *She moved past her grief, at least long enough to connect with her grandmother.* The notion made his heart a little warmer, helping fight the chill of the surrounding Lost Ones.

"Now then, what *have* you been up to? Why didn't you call me? Oh!" she gasped, prying one of Izabella's hands loose to look into her clenched hands. "Have you been off sneaking churros again, little one? You know we have them at home."

"No, Grandma." Izabella laughed a weak reply, as now her grandmother took over wiping tears and makeup from her face. "That nice man over there." She pointed at Miguel. "He helped me when I was sad and gave me a churro. He said I should go talk to you."

"Oh, such a nice man." The elderly woman nodded. "Maybe you should marry him."

"Grandma!"

Grandma cackled to herself. "I'm just playing with you, churro. But come along, we should get home. I have supper almost ready."

With Izabella for support, she turned toward the door, then looked at Miguel.

"Thank you," Grandma said with genuine appreciation. "Thank you for helping my little churro come home."

"Good luck, Miguel." Izabella smiled.

Miguel's grin faded. *I didn't tell her my name. How did she…* A thought dawned on him. *I became part of her celebration. She needed my name to thank me, to move on.* A warm tear ran down his cheek.

"Thank you for coming," Madame Muertos chimed, giving a last wave to the parting duo.

"You're still here," the aged woman growled. "Shouldn't you be getting that door fixed? Lazy girl!"

Muertos smiled, more out of custom than friendliness. “Of course, I… live to serve.” Her voice trailed off into a groan. She followed them to the door, waving as they walked onto the outside landing. “Okay, bye-bye, have a wonderful trip.” Her tone shot up in falsetto as she rose on her tiptoes to ensure the door was fully closed before turning.

For a moment, her eyes met Miguel’s. The green fire that burned there was only present on the very edges. Muertos nodded but then shook her head. Was she happy with what happened or disappointed to see Miguel still here? Muertos had seemed confused by the elderly woman’s sudden appearance. What did that mean for Miguel and the time he had left?

Looking at his notepad, Miguel smiled at the word *churro* written at the top.

There was a heavy thud as someone filled the seat beside him. It was another Lost One, this spirit a man covered in tattoos, dressed in a worn leather jacket and pants with zippers all over but none that led to pockets. His head was clean-shaven, and every place that could be pierced had metal jutting through it. There was an aura of pain and menace about the silver-blue man.

"Ay," he roared, anger crackling in his voice. "You think all that is true? All that bric-a-brac you were telling that lady? You believe her granny wanted her back so bad she'd come here to get her?"

"Yes," Miguel replied with a cautious grin.

The man glared back at him, squeezing his fist hard enough to pop his knuckles. His breathing came in short, agitated spurts. Like Izabella, his face was set in a powerful emotional state. Instead of her sorrowful expression, his was one of rage. His silver-blue body shook as he examined Miguel.

"Yeah? Is that so? Then I got something to ask you, since you seem to be the man with *all* the answers. You think you can answer *my* question, Mr. Answers?"

Miguel leaned back in his chair. "Okay…"

Tension built in his chest, and the man drew back to his full height. He opened his mouth, releasing a puff of air and a foul odor. Miguel gagged. *It seems we don't have breath mints here.*

The man reached out, grabbing Miguel by the wrist to hold his attention. The tattooed figure snorted, snot and tears running down his face. "Then can we talk to you? Can you help us?"

Around them, Lost Ones stepped out of the shadows. No longer floating in the distance, they raced forward, their individual voices merging into a cacophony of sounds. Every one of them watched Miguel, calling out for his attention. There were dozens of them, perhaps more. It was hard to tell with their silver-blue glow filling the space.

Holding up his pen, Miguel gave it a click. "Start at the beginning," he said, motioning for the man to sit. Then, seeing that the newcomer had already taken a seat, Miguel ran his hand through his hair in a poor attempt to not look foolish. Thankfully, the leather-clad man did not seem to notice, instead wiping his nose on his sleeve with far more noise than he needed to. He took a blubbering, beleaguered breath. "Well, it all started when…"

Chapter 13: Closing Time

For what felt like hours, the straggling spirits sat and spoke to Miguel. To some he gave his opinion. With others he shared a drink. He wondered where the drinks were coming from with the bar closed and Raquel off duty, but he would give a silent nod toward the recreation rooms and think of the Marias.

He took notes as best as he could, not for any kind of case file, but because it seemed appropriate and helped with the quicker-speaking spirits. Others said their piece and drew their own conclusions by the end of their stories. No matter who it was, however, all of them thanked him, whether with a hug, a nod, or a few kind words. Each story ended with the stuck entrance to the bar slamming open and a loved one entering, although after the first few arrivals, Muertos no longer appeared to greet the newcomers, and Miguel wondered what else she was doing.

After Izabella and her grandmother, Miguel's second-favorite reunion was the tattooed man being collected by a small calico kitten he called Meow-ster Answers.

“I suppose everyone needs a little push in the right direction sometimes,” Miguel mused, watching when the last spirit faded away. For a moment, he remembered how Raquel shoved him from the bar and winced at the memory of that pain. “I guess help doesn’t always feel good.”

Wiping the sweat from his brow, Miguel let out a deep breath that echoed in the space. The room had changed again, shrinking back for a more intimate gathering. *Is that for me?* He wondered as he rubbed the tablecloth. The overhead lights went off with a loud click, leaving only the candles at the center of each table for illumination. As he turned, he could no longer make out the stage or the bar. Juan Pedro and Raquel were gone, back to wherever they resided during the daylight hours.

The staircase remained, which meant he was not alone.

“And so, we come to the end of another night.” Madame Muertos said. Glancing over his shoulder. It surprised Miguel to see that she was not standing behind him, no longer playing her favorite trick.

"One guest left," she continued in a droll tone. As a tabletop candle went out, Miguel could just make out Muertos's shape before the area went dark. A moment later, another candle fizzled out, and another table went dark. "What are we to do with you, Miguel?"

Miguel shuffled his assortment of notes from his conversations with the Lost Ones. He knew there was no reason to tidy up—the paper would vanish when no longer needed—but he needed something to busy his attention and help him avoid meeting Madame Muertos's eyes.

There was something different about her. The usual warmth and playful energy were replaced with an icy stillness. He recalled how he had once thought of her as the center of a pool of rippling water. Miguel now saw her not as the still center, but as the stone that disturbed the lake's surface, one that sank slow and steady into the depths. He could see his breath forming into small clouds before him. The room grew colder.

"Tell me," she whispered, snuffing out another candle. "Did you enjoy yourself? Did you find a reason to move on, a reason for being, Miguel?"

“No.” He sighed, trying his best to appear calm. “No,” he repeated, steeling his nerves. “I spent the night distracted, celebrating the lives of others and talking to staff. You could say I was too busy being a busybody to enjoy myself.”

“A busybody,” she mused, stressing the last word. “Interesting word choice in a land where bodies would be corpses.”

He coughed out a polite, if weak, laugh. “Yes, well. It was a distracting night. I had the Lost Ones watching me, which was creepy, and then there was the time I spent with the Marias… not to mention Raquel and Juan Pedro. You and I even danced. The entire night felt like a series of distractions.”

“Well, I am sorry to hear that.” Muertos sighed, her voice accented by the smoldering of a candle flame. “But a Death Night Festival *is* a kind of distraction. Distracting the deceased from their fate so they can move on.”

“Plus, I kept having this strange memory pop up. I could never quite figure it out, and it got me thinking the same question over and over.”

“Miguel.” Her voice was somber. “You’re rambling. What was it? What was the question you had? Speak.”

"Well, I thought I knew you." He laughed.

"Everyone knows me at some point. I told you that when you first arrived: all come through my home."

"No, not like that. I thought I knew you during my life, that we interacted or met face to face. But how? How would I know you?"

"How indeed," she replied, putting out another candle. As it fizzled out, Miguel noted that only one remained: the candle at his table.

"Last chance, Miguel. Ask the question you want. There is little time left, and 'closing time is still closing time.'" She echoed Raquel's words from earlier, but not with the same tone or with any of her usual humor.

Drawing in an icy breath, he spoke. "Madame Muertos, are you… are you my mother?"

Her voice sounded like wind through old trees, wispy and forlorn. “Oh, Miguel. Is that how you’ve seen me this evening? A reflection of your madre? That is truly an unfair card for fate to play. No, I am not your madre.” Madame Muertos stepped from the shadows and into the dull illumination coming from Miguel’s table so he could see her.

No longer did he see the image of his mother, but a spectral figure made of silver-blue light. Her mask of face paint no longer made her look like a person dressed as a skeleton. Instead, it humanized what lay beneath. The green flame in her eyes had been extinguished, replaced by cold gray orbs. *Is this how everyone else has seen her all night?*

“But I remember you. When I look at you, I remember her face, her smile, and how she held me as a baby. I’m reminded of all the times I wished my mother were there in my life. If you are not her, why would I remember her?”

"You saw what you needed for your festival, Miguel." For a moment, the warmth she had possessed wove its way into her expression, taking some of the chill from her appearance. But it soon faltered, swallowed by the surrounding darkness. Miguel wondered if she would reach out to him, would show comfort as she had previously that night, but instead, she clasped her hands and bowed her head. "Also, you remember me with your mother, because I was there"."

"What? I thought you were married to the Grim Reaper, not that you *were* him."

"I am not, and he really hates that nickname. He says it was a phase, but no one lets him forget it." She cut herself off, a soft chuckling rattling from her lips. "I apologize. You have little time left, and here I am rambling about my husband's fashion and social appearance."

With a wave of her hand, images swirled in the air beside her. “Let me show you.” The images coalesced into the blue rooms. “So often, I spent my nights in what would become Azul’s halls. It was a quiet place, always away from the parties. I loved to look over the children, as I could never have one. For a moment each night, I felt like I had children of my own. Like any parent, I eventually had to watch them go. I am, after all, the guide for the dead.”

The image shifted, and Miguel saw Muertos and another skeletal figure talking. Based on their gestures, they appeared to be in the throes of an argument. “I longed to see a living child, to see them experience life itself, but my husband would not allow it. He dared tell me not to walk the land of the living so frivolously. But I could not be stopped. I would not be denied. One night, when he left for his work, I followed.” She stopped, blue light flaring against her silver eyes. “Does it surprise you, Miguel, that I could avoid even Death’s detection?”

Miguel shook his head, and she laughed, but it was a sound without mirth.

The scene changed again, and now she appeared to be walking through a hospital. Despite her spectral appearance, she gave off an excited energy. Perhaps it was the way she walked, with a bounce and twirl, but it reminded Miguel of his own wife.

"I walked a hospital, seeing so many little ones have their first meetings with their family." She let out a warm rasp that Miguel took as a joyous sigh. "They were all so happy." The swirling images were a vibrant wash of colors. Looking at the pictures was nearly blinding, but still Miguel watched with equal parts morbid curiosity and wonder.

"But then my husband found me," she hissed, and the colors fell away, leaving only a silver-blue outline to the images. "Where Death appears, people die. My presence brought him to your room. The random hand of fate decided who would be called. I want you to understand, Miguel, we did not choose who would be claimed. That is something far beyond either of our power. We fulfill our roles. Failure to do so has consequences." She stopped, swirling the images with a bony finger. "You have not seen true hurt until you see it in Death's eyes. That night, he forbade me from ever following him again, and I accepted my punishment. Here I have remained, in my home, greeting the departed. I threw myself into my work, ensuring it was ready for guests, removing anything that could be in their way."

"The Lost Ones," he whispered. "That's when you started…"

"My sisters said it was too much, that I was taking my grief out on others, but I think I was helping them. They had to move on." Muertos waved a hand. "They left, and I continued the work alone."

"If I may, you're not alone. You have help. Raquel and the Marias for starters," he offered.

She gave another humorless laugh.

"What about Juan Pedro, then?"

"He made me laugh, which brought me joy for a short time." She nodded in agreement. "To put so much passion and work into such a silly pun. I allow him to remain until the joke is told to its audience."

"Wait, that proves that not all who can't move on have to become Lost Ones. If you've allowed him to continue, why not others?"

She turned on him. "You think I have the time to attend to every life? I give them the chance to celebrate the life they were given while I watch from beyond. You would ask me to give them even more?"

"Perhaps I could help. I mean, I helped several spirits tonight. I could do it again." His heart raced a bit. "At least until I see my wife again. Give me a chance to meet my son. You could consider it an extension of my Death Night Festival. A chance for me to be a part of their celebrations since my celebration went so poorly."

Her sunken eyes blazed, silver-blue fire crackling beneath spectral skin. "Are you saying you did not celebrate, Miguel?" She stepped forward, now at an arm's length from him. His table's candle flickered, diminishing in her presence.

"No, I 'couldn't," Miguel replied, grasping at anything that could keep the conversation going and keep the candle lit. He was not sure what would happen if it went out but felt it would not be good. "Knowing I was dead meant I 'couldn't enjoy the moment"."

"'Couldn't enjoy it"?" she scoffed. "You did not enjoy cake with new friends"?"

"That hardly seems like my celebration. I was just a piece to their event"."

A growl emerged from somewhere deep in her chest, and she leaned forward, her skull visage before him as her words came in a quick barrage. "And did you not watch an angel soar? Walk a world of entertainment on a bolt of green lightning? Did you not get to experience nearly drowning in the depths of your own greatest pains? Mr. Miguel, did you not quite literally drink more than a house?" There was a hiss as she rose. "I'll admit, getting my home drunk is an impressive feat. While I'd be interested to know how you did it, I can find out from Violeta Maria later."

Miguel swallowed. *Does she not know about the flask?*

She paced, her voice angry as she listed the night's events. "Did we not share a dance? You danced with Death's wife. Did not my home mimic your happiest moments?"

"But those were all with the staff. I 'wasn't really talking with the departed. Is that even a fair Death Night Festival? You said no one dies alone, and it seems tonight was just me."

"No? You met many spirits of the departed tonight. Did I not provide you closure by letting you meet your own killer? Letting you decide your vengeance? Do you know how many people would wish for such a thing? You came into my home specially, Miguel, so I gave you a special evening to help you on your way. To leave this place behind and experience the hereafter." Cold electricity crackled in her eyes as her voice rose. "Did you not, just an hour ago, perform before the assembled dead to the adoration of everyone on my stage?"

"And 'didn't I pay all that back to you by helping everyone with their celebrations? Look around you, Madame Muertos. There is no one else here. The Lost Ones have all moved on. 'They've found their place"." Miguel's stomach dropped at his own words. *So much for negotiating any more time.*

Muertos whirled on him, the surrounding air roiling and churning. "You would dare infer I am incapable of doing my job? In my home?"

She resumed her place before him, then reached out to the tiny flame. "Enough. I have given you all I can. We have reached an impasse. That much is clear." Her hand descended. "I am sorry, Miguel, but it is time."

That much is clear. The words echoed in his mind.

Miguel smiled. "Please, before you do, one last drink? My throat is dry, and I would like to face my fate with clarity."

She stopped. "The bar is closed. The night is over."

"Madame Muertos"," Miguel said with a polite nod. "I beg your pardon, but I was talking to someone who offered me clarity"." There was a faint clunk as a small object landed on the table between them. A flask. More specifically, Violeta Maria's flask of source liquid.

Muertos leaned back, curious at the object in his hand. "What is that?"

"Join me for a drink?" he asked, opening the cap. "We could share. Or perhaps get some glasses." No sooner had the words left his mouth than two glasses appeared. One shone brightly. The other had a smudge running its length. A blink later, the marked glass was replaced.

He poured the contents into the two glasses until the flask was empty. “There,” he said with satisfaction, taking one glass and handing the other to Muertos. “Be careful, it is potent”.”

“A drink with Death?” she mused, swirling the contents of her glass. “I have never eaten or drunk with a guest before. That is more my sisters’ method, but since this has been an unusual night, I suppose one drink will not hurt.” Madame Muertos raised her glass in a toast. “As they say, it’s your funeral.”

Miguel beamed, returning her gesture. “I prefer to think it’s one for the road”.”

As the golden liquid raced down his throat, Miguel recalled how Violeta Maria described it. She had called it “everything,” but with a second helping, Miguel thought that was not quite right. The drink was possibility—it was choices, everything that made up life. As it coursed through his body, Miguel understood why Raquel portioned out the drink and customized it. The distilled drinks and food limited its effect to the choices a person made in life, refining it through their memories.

Through the rush of memories and experiences, both his own and those borrowed from people he knew, Miguel peered at Madame Muertos. She had gone rigid, the empty, upturned glass still held to her lips.

Then Muertos changed. It was like she was crying, but not in the way a person cried. Tears did not fall from her eyes. Instead, the colored decorations and spectral energy of her body flowed upward and inward into her vacant eye sockets. Starting with a trickle, the streams increased their speed until the sound of moving liquid roared like a waterfall. The sound continued to build until it exploded with a blinding light and deafening sound.

For several moments, Miguel could not hear or see anything. He was aware of his surroundings, but only just. *Focus*, he told himself, unable to tell if he was thinking or speaking aloud. Eventually, he could see and hear again, hazy images and high-pitched squealing sounds. He continued to force himself to breathe until the room stabilized.

Madame Muertos sat beside him; her appearance shifted back to how he had first seen her at the start of the evening. She lay draped over the table, a sickly pallor to her face. “I think I threw up,” she groaned, fighting back a convulsion from her stomach. “What was in that drink?”

Hearing her gulp, Miguel fought to control his own stomach. “That was a shot of source material.” He winced as he tried to sit up. Then, failing at that, he continued to slouch in his chair. “You got to experience everything, all at once.”

Something moved at the fringes of his vision. Others moved about the room. Miguel groaned, “How long were we out? Is it opening already?”

Muertos rolled faced-down on the table. “No,” she moaned. “I told you, I threw up. These are the Lost Ones I have consumed before. That drink made them flare up in my stomach. Now they will wander all over again.”

“I can help. I know I can. I helped others tonight, and I can do it again.”

She tried lifting her head but could only flop onto the side of her face. Madame Muertos cast him a confused glance. Her voice was tired, and she rasped out her question. “What makes you so special to think you can guide the dead when even I could not?”

Miguel made a weak chuckle, the motion sending a wave of pain through his aching body. “Well, I was a life coach.”

Madame Muertos let out a deep, hearty laugh that started at her core and soon shook her entire body. As she did, the room came alive with lights, decorations, and tables. She rose on weary legs, looking ready to collapse at any moment but always righting herself before she did. “*A life coach*, in the land of the deceased.” She clapped and lightning crackled around her hands. “Now that is something I have not heard before.”

She stopped, rolling her hand toward him. “Very well, Miguel. I relent. You have given me, Madame Muertos, a clarity I did not know I was missing. You’ve helped the lost.” She accented that last word, showing she wasn’t just addressing the Lost Ones. “And you’ve proven your tenacity to me.” She laughed again, this time more controlled and proper, then held out a hand. “Do you accept?”

Without a moment's hesitation, Miguel accepted. His hand tingled, and he quivered at her touch but otherwise felt unchanged. "So what happens now? Do I help these people?"

Muertos looked at the spirits. While possessing a silver sheen, they milled about the room, some venturing out onto the empty patio. "Not today," she said with a slow breath. "These souls are confused and will need your aid, I think, but not right now. Our work is at night. For now, let them wander the house. Seeing behind the curtain did wonders for you. Perhaps it can do the same for them. No, right now, we have another matter to attend to that is more urgent." She gestured to an open door, which glowed with a burning white light. "The irrevocable part of joining my employ. You must accept your fate and complete moving on."

A familiar tugging sensation drew Miguel toward the door, reminding him of the presence that drew him into Madame Muertos's home at the start of the evening.

She smiled. "Even the house wants you here, Miguel."

As he reached the edge of the light, his legs locked. Even standing before the open door, he could see nothing on the other side. Miguel swallowed, turning to the hostess. "Will you go with me?"

"Of course," she whispered. "As I told you earlier, no one moves on alone." With her steady hands on his shoulders, Miguel and Madame Muertos stepped toward the light.

Chapter 14: Stepping into the Light

Everything that followed stepping through that door came in a blur of rushed motions, light, and noises. They entered a room of brilliant white light, the illumination blinding him. He heard Muertos let out a faint laugh before moving away from him.

When his vision adjusted, he was in a simple reception hall. Nothing as fancy or grand as the Death Night Festival had been, but still decorated well for the occasion.

His blurry eyes scanned the room, and Miguel recalled how he felt when he first arrived: dizzy, disoriented, and confused. *Am I starting tonight all over?* Above him on the far wall was a large yellow banner with red letters. Underneath it was a multitiered cake that was taller than any of them. *Focus*, he told himself. *You should be good at that by now.* He read the banner multiple times until he comprehended its meaning. With that understanding, time snapped back to its normal flow, and he could see and hear what was happening around him.

The banner read, *Welcome aboard, Miguel!*

Everyone was cheering and applauding, their attention resting upon him.

Something firm bumped into his ribs. Miguel recognized the specific way it hurt and turned to the only person who could make a playful gesture hurt so much. "Raquel," he moaned.

The bartender laughed, wrapping one arm around his neck before falling against him. Unlike everyone else in the room, she did not have a champagne flute in her hand. Instead, Raquel held an entire bottle, which she seemed to have almost emptied while they waited.

"What is this…?"

"A welcome party." Azul Maria yawned and handed him a flute. "It's been so long since we had a party or anything to celebrate. It's so nice to have a reason to relax." Azul took a sip from her glass, starting to stretch midway through her drink but steadying herself a moment before anything spilled on the floor.

"A party," Miguel repeated, his brain still processing everything going on. Sure enough, every member of the staff was there. Juan Pedro and his band stood in a cleared corner, alternating between drinking and tuning their instruments as they waited for their cue. *Even after a full night of performing, they are still ready for more.*

Violeta and Lima Maria were by the large, layered cake. Lima was busy setting out place sets of utensils and plates, tilting her head to examine her work and then switching the orientation of their layout. Violeta attempted to place napkins beside each plate but was forced to reset them after Lima's erratic utensil placement. This began an endless cycle of one sister correcting for the other.

Muertos shifted Raquel from Miguel to Azul, who did not seem to notice having someone clinging onto her. Azul strode to a chair, setting Raquel in an open seat before taking another for herself. She moved with the practiced motions of a tired parent.

With Miguel visible again, Muertos turned to address the room. "Everyone," she called, drawing all eyes to her and Miguel. "Thank you so much for coming tonight." A few murmurs came from the crowd, and he was surprised Raquel had not made a remark.

Little victories, he thought with a mild smile.

“This was a fantastic Death Night Festival, one that I had not thought we would ever see again. I want to thank you all for your efforts.” She paused, drawing Miguel up beside her. “Tonight, we had *no* Lost Ones.” Murmurs came from the crowd, a mix of approval and concern. “They all moved on,” she added. At this, everyone clapped, and there were a few whistles.

Miguel rubbed his ear. Someone whistled with the sound of metal scraping on glass. *One guess who that is.* He turned to Lima Maria and nodded in her direction. For an instant, he saw a smile flicker across her face. Then she turned to the table, distracted by something no one else could notice. Violeta reached out a hand to steady her sister, a gentle nudge to return Lima’s focus to the speech.

After a few moments, Madame Muertos raised her hands to silence them. “Yes, I know. I am as surprised as the rest of you. After all that has happened, to see everyone move on… well, it’s not something I thought I would be *alive* to see.” She grinned, expecting a laugh from the crowd. No one laughed. She sighed. “Even I cannot remember the last time that happened, and I’ve been here for as long as… Well, a long time.”

"But still as lovely as ever," Juan Pedro shouted, helping her recover her momentum.

She pointed at him in acknowledgment, a smile on her face. "That being said, it was not through any of our efforts it happened. No, tonight's special situation has warranted me bringing on someone new." Muertos moved Miguel so he stood in front of her, the full attention of the gathered staff upon him. "Allow me to be the first to welcome our newest employee. He will be taking on a role we have been missing for some time now. Miguel, life coach for the Lost Ones!"

The room erupted in cheers, screams, and applause. Miguel heard at least one champagne flute shatter from the sheer volume. When the cheers and clapping died away, no one moved. Instead, they waited and watched him, as if expecting to see something.

Or hear something. He swallowed, recognizing this setup. *A speech, really? Maybe I should take my chances outside…* He tried to step away, but Muertos blocked his path with a gentle hand on his shoulder. Miguel sighed and nodded to the crowd. "Thank you, everyone. I—"

“Yeah, Miguel,” Raquel shouted, misreading the room. Muertos stepped away with a weak laugh and pried the bottle from Raquel’s grip. Surprised by the sudden emptiness of her hand, Raquel moaned in disappointment.

“Yes, well,” he continued, “I don’t know what to say after that. I have no speech prepared. If I did, it wouldn’t be exceptionally good.”

“Great start,” Juan Pedro shouted, drawing a laugh from the band.

Lima clapped, her hands disappearing as they continued to get faster until they were little more than a blur. Violeta stopped her sister before the whirring hands blew all the napkins from the table. She shook her head, letting Lima know it was not yet time. With a twitch, she stopped.

“Joking aside, thank you. Thank you, everyone, for making tonight a grand Death Night Festival for me. I hope to make you all proud, for as long as we are together.”

Miguel drifted around the room, making small talk and accepting welcomes from various individuals. While the night had gotten him used to crowds, those gatherings had been Death Night Festivals where things happened and were over in what felt like an instant. Here, time moved more slowly, more calmly, and more at his speed. The rush of the night moving moment to moment was gone, replaced by a relaxed calm as everyone chatted about the night's oddities. It was strange to see so many faces he did not recognize, which he supposed belonged to staff who worked behind the scenes or assisted as required. As he met more and more of them, Miguel started to understand how much more there was to learn about this place. There was more to the afterlife than just talking to people.

His wandering led him up to the largest tiered cake he had ever seen. Each tier was decorated to reflect his Death Night Festival, from the bottom tier showing his arrival to the top where he and a tiny candy Muertos stood before a pretzel door. Seeing his evening depicted in cake form was impressive, but also unnerving, as it meant someone had been watching him. He shuddered as he considered what the cake *could* have looked like if things had gone differently.

I have never been intimidated by a cake before.

"Do you want a slice?" Lima chimed, appearing in a jittering whirl of green. She waved a large knife as she spoke, and Miguel breathed a sigh of relief when Violeta snatched it from her hands.

"I'll do the cutting, Lima," Violeta explained. "Remember last time?"

"But we found the hand," Lima Maria said.

"Most of it." Azul yawned, picking up a plate and taking a bite, either unaware or uncaring that there was no cake on her plate.

Violeta Maria said nothing, moving the knife away. "We will try next time, sister."

"Here, let me do it," Raquel boomed, staggering into the conversation.

"You are way too drunk, Raquel," Violeta snapped. "I'd trust you with a knife even less than Lima!"

"Hey!" Lima and Raquel replied in offended unison.

Miguel took the knife from Violeta before the scene could escalate. "Since it is my cake and all, I should cut it." He made a few quick slices, impressed by how easily the knife cut the cake.

Once he had two slices, he held them out to Violeta and Raquel. “See, piece of cake.”

Raquel reached out, taking the plate without removing her eyes from Violeta Maria. Her red eyes twinkled, and she caught the look.

Violeta’s eyes narrowed to slits. “Oh, you wouldn’t dare—” Before she could finish, Raquel smashed the cake into her face. She gasped, mortified, and scooped chunks of frosting and cake away to clear her vision.

Raquel laughed until she snorted, while Violeta took the other plate and returned the favor. Blinded, the angel reached out for anything to throw and pulled free an entire layer from the center of the cake. Without the middle support, the upper layers collapsed atop Miguel, the Marias, and Muertos, who had stepped forward to remove the knife from the field of battle. As her arm moved backward, the freed tier broke, peppering the rest of the crowd in a shower of frosting, candy decorations, and moist cake.

“Children,” Muertos hissed. A strand of frosting hung from the rim of her hat, waggling as she spoke as if the sugary concoction was also chastising everyone. Miguel covered his mouth, trying to stifle a laugh, but the lady of the house turned her cold eyes to him. “You find something funny, Miguel?”

“I didn’t mean…” Miguel stopped as Muertos tossed the frosting strand from her hand into his face. She laughed, a haunting melody. Raquel and Violeta each grabbed a section of cake and moved to opposite sides of the room, tossing frosted dessert like snowballs at each other. Those who had been hit joined in to get their revenge, which sparked more thrown cake. Alliances and betrayals came and went as the room descended into cream-covered chaos and high-pitched laughter. Juan Pedro kept the band playing, adjusting their music to mimic the surrounding scene. This lasted until a layer of red frosting hit Juan Pedro’s suit, and it forced him to join the battle to avenge his fallen friend.

When it was over, Miguel noted that not much of the cake had been eaten. *At least not eaten by choice. I wonder if that was the point of making it so big.* With no more cake to destroy, everyone set down plates, soldiers lowering their shields at the end of a battle. Covered in frosting, cake crumbles, and smiles, they set about cleaning the room with laughter and good humor.

"This was an interesting welcome," Miguel said to Muertos, bobbing his head at the destroyed party. "Thank you."

"I need no thanks. You earned this. Plus, I am a firm believer that hard work requires a reward of fierce play." She looked around the room, regarding her employees. "It was good to celebrate with them again. It reminded me of old times, like when my sister…" She paused, a smile creasing her face. "Perhaps another time for that, yes?"

"Yes, another time." Miguel scooped a large portion of cake. "But that is two cakes I destroyed in one night. I suppose I should apologize to this Chef person."

“I’d say you’ve had enough excitement for one night, Miguel. Leave something for tomorrow night.” She hefted two bags of trash with ease and gave him a pleasant nod. “Our work is done for now. Until tomorrow night, Miguel. Good day.”

Miguel nodded back at her, watching the others disappear out the door one by one. As he tied up his trash bag, he allowed himself to reflect on the night and all the things he had seen and done. How he had danced with Death, watched an angel race, performed with the band, communed with spirits of the house, and guided the Lost Ones to their path. *Not bad for a dead man*. He laughed. Stopping at the door, he picked up a stray glass, noticing it was still full. Before he followed the others, he raised the glass in salute to the empty room.

“One for the road.”

www.ingramcontent.com/pod-product-compliance
Lightning Source LLC
LaVergne TN
LVHW010606100826
845148LV00014B/2873
* 9 7 8 1 7 3 6 0 5 3 8 0 5 *